FLOWER OF THE ROCKIES

QUEEN OF THE ROCKIES SERIES BOOK 4

ANGELA BREIDENBACH

FLOWER OF THE ROCKIES

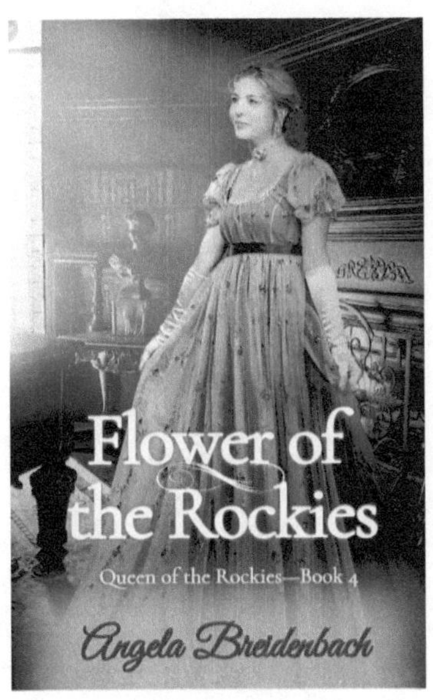

ISBN eBook: 978-1-957132-01-3

ISBN 13 Pbk: 978-1-957132-02-0

ISBN Large Print: 978-1-957132-03-7

Angela E Breidenbach, LLC

Published by Gems Books

Contact for questions and permissions:
angela@angelabreidenbach.com

Breidenbach, Angela

Flower of the Rockies by Angela Breidenbach

1. Fiction—Historical 2. Fiction—Religious

This book is a work of fiction set in a real location. Any reference to historical figures, places, or events, whether fictional or actual, is a fictional representation.

Biblical verses used in this work of fiction are taken from the (RV) Revised Version 1885 and are Public Domain.

Published in the United States of America (Missoula, MT)

No one knows the real Emmalee Warren — Just what they want from her. Can she leave her past behind?

I am enjoying these books that are teaching me more about Montana through a sweet story. I highly recommend reading the authors notes in the back of the book. It really makes the story come to life. I highly recommend this series. The author has a talent for weaving facts about Montana and this era into a beautiful fiction story.

— Donna Feyen, MoreThanAReview.com

What a cast of characters! Unveiling Emmalee Warren's hurts and scars drew me into the story and made me want to get to know her more. Then comes Richard Lewis who sees past her past and then gently and patiently shows her her value. With redemption at its core, *Flower of the Rockies* was a memorable historical romance that touched my heart.

— Susan G. Mathis, bestselling author of The Thousand Islands Brides Series

INTRODUCTION

Flower of the Rockies was an interesting book for me
to write because in the brainstorming of the character I realized a parallel existed between my childhood and hers. Emmalee's illiteracy with letters
became an emotional internal struggle for me when I
realized she mirrored my illiteracy with people
through my childhood and into my early adult years.
I've set her age in the story at about the same age as
I began to understand how to better connect rela-
tionally. The analogy deepened my writing experience and connection to her.

As Miss Emmie, her alter ego, she had a hard-
ened exterior in order to live out the sacrifice for her
family in a way she could emotionally handle. But
the pain in crossing over into "acceptable" society
brought Emmalee face-to-face with her demons. In a

similar manner, I had to face mine as I learned to trust others and build deeper friendships rather than hold people off at a distance.

Different than Emmalee's situation, I hadn't learned how to "read" people because of growing up with a mentally ill mother and an alcoholic stepfather. In Emmalee's world, when her mother died, and her father later disappeared circumstance left her responsible for two younger siblings. In the 1800s, and as a young teen, she had no protection or choice. She could only rely on herself and her limited knowledge of the world. Though not the same situation, the lack of emotional and physical support created a trust and connection problem for me. Writing this story allowed me to show that God uses ALL of our experiences for our good and to create some amazing testimony. We're able to help others who have experienced life's unfairness. There's a beautiful redemption when we can comfort and come alongside people who need support and understanding because we've been there and felt the pain, too.

Sure, no one wants to experience pain. But none of us escape it. I want to use those experiences to spread hope, courage, love, joy, and bring peace to other people who are on similar paths. Finding that the past became a wealth of wisdom changes how I view it and the future. Courage, confidence, and the ability to grow into the person God intends helps me to love that little girl who had to make choices that hurt to survive. I hope in reading *Flower of the Rockies,* that you'll be able to view your past hurts as a well of wisdom and come to a beautiful peace that offers others a safe place to rest.

CHAPTER 1

Helena, Montana
June 1894

Infamous.

She couldn't walk down a street in town without drawing attention—even fully clothed. No matter that she wore widow's garb for a year. Longer than most in a town where men outnumbered women since its inception. No matter that she never looked at a man, other than her husband in two years. The men knew who she was, and they stared. Therefore, the women knew, and they ostracized. But they didn't know she'd just been fleeced by a scoundrel! Would they care if they did?

Emmalee Warren seethed as the layered ruffles of her cotton skirt swished around her white kid boots like the summer windstorms blowing through the passes. Woe to another man that ever crossed her path! Only one had ever been kind. Unfortunately, every gold-digger within a day's ride wanted to stake a claim on her, since Charles died in the cave in. Silver mines meant nothing these days. But owning a gold mine… if her past occupation hadn't already marked her, being the heiress to a working gold mine brought men out like ants to a sugar pile. She didn't need any of the pests. What she did need, right now, was a good lawyer!

The grocer's shop door opened, spilling a youngster and his mama into her path. The woman's smile flared as she made eye contact.

Emmalee smiled back.

"Oh!" And as fleeting, the good woman's smile faltered. "Quickly son, move quickly." Her words not even whispered as she snagged his hand and tugged the boy away.

Emmalee masked her disappointment under the wide brim of the elegant rose covered hat. It'd been the first smile she'd seen in a long time. "Excuse me." She moved aside, allowing the mother and child to pass onto the sidewalk. Emmalee would not lower herself to treat another poorly. But after attempting for two years to be courteous to respectable folks, what more could she do? No one knew her or bothered, unless they wanted something. No one cared that she wanted a fresh start.

That she didn't want to go back from whence she came.

The woman covered the little boy's eyes. "We don't notice people like that, Erwin."

"Why Mama? She's pretty." His little brows furrowed. "Why don't we notice people like that?"

"Shh, don't be rude, son."

People like that. Emmalee blinked back a sharp sting behind her eyelids. First it had been her body, and now the money and mine her husband left behind. On such a sunny day, the scent of green grass in the breeze off the mountains, her heart suffered a drought near as bad as the Great Plains experienced these last few years. What was it yesterday's unexpected caller had said as he'd offered the last in a long line of inappropriate proposals?

"I shore liked the way that lacey dress fit them there bosoms." The lout's words beat the same drum she'd heard for years. In what way did any man think lewdness was a compliment?

She shuddered. Chicago Joe's Coliseum Theatre promoted that distinctive fashion statement, an all lace dressing gown that clung to her curvaceous figure. Men flocked to see her. She forced the memory away shoving it behind a wall in her mind.

Emmalee glanced over her shoulder with a pang in her empty womb. What would she have said in the other woman's place? The mother kept a guiding hand clamped on the boy's neck, making it impossible for him to sneak a peek at a woman who didn't deserve to be seen. The cowlick in his caramel brown hair popped between his mother's gloved fingers.

No, that kind of persnickety behavior wouldn't have been a Warren family value. But then Charles Warren's mother had also been a lady of a certain profession. He'd been sent to the best schools she could afford. He didn't share a distaste of those less fortunate. A fond smile crossed Emmalee's lips. She missed the way he'd read the newspaper to her after dinner. Without him, she floated in a disconnected life like a lost soul, not fitting in anywhere anymore.

Twenty-five. A little too late to wish for a child that wouldn't be in Emmalee's future. With no husband, and the doctor's report, well, she couldn't wallow there now. She needed a lawyer, not a ridiculous pretense she'd ever have a family that people like her didn't deserve.

A one-year marriage couldn't create respectability or a baby for her husband. Not after being a well-known soiled dove for the most famous madam in Montana, Chicago Joe— the woman Emmalee couldn't forgive. Josephine had the blessing of owning property and had somehow finagled her way into respectability in Helena's society — that is until the 1885 ordinance pushed them all into the shadows. If the silver crash hadn't happened last July, Emmalee might have never been let go from her lease. But Charles struck gold instead of silver. He offered cash for his favorite dalliance in the last bordello left to Chicago Joe. Cash the madam badly needed to settle debts. Cash that freed one popular Miss Emmie, Darling of the Queen City of the Rockies, from an occupation that awarded a lone girl survival in the unforgiving frontier, albeit also the expectation of a shorter lifespan.

Banking would be much easier if she'd been allowed to get more than a third-grade education. As would reading thick contracts, like the one stuffed in the envelope inside her reticule with the bank statement showing a measly hundred dollars instead of a thousand. How could she know the partner Charles trusted meant to fleece her? How did Chicago Joe succeed when she couldn't read or write either? But then that was the argument—education. Who needed a seductress that could read and write? Her job skills were more of the… physical nature. Scratching a name was more than enough in her profession. Too bad Miss Emmie couldn't even do that right!

A cowboy hooked a double take from his saddle, then reined his gelding into a fast redirection. The roan stamped his front hooves and squealed displeasure before settling into obedience. "Ho there, little lady!" He reined away from a carriage and came back for another pass. "Miss Ellie, I heard you was available agin."

She ignored him, walking on. Ellie, for pity's sake. At least he could have gotten her name right!

"I jes wanna talk." He called from nearly the middle of the street.

Picking up her pace, Emmalee averted her eyes and pressed her lips together at his transparent persistence. She refused to acknowledge the commotion he'd created or the stares from anyone, man or woman. She also refused to be caught in yet another annoying conversation professing undying love from a no-good money-grubber. Even an uneducated woman knew enough to avoid a lout drawing unwanted attention on the street. She switched her parasol into the other hand, blocking the annoyance from view.

Although some of the men pressing for her affections may have been customers, they were still unwelcome. Miss Emmie had quit that life. To lock away the past, she'd need to sell her home and move away—start over where no one knew Miss Emmie. The padlock on the iron cage around her heart could only be accessed from the inside—the key conveniently buried deep. She'd certainly learned that while under Chicago Joe's tutelage. And she refused to go back. But if her bank account didn't have the funds, thanks to a dishonest mining partner, what would she do to survive?

Emmalee closed her parasol and grasped the door handle of the Goodkind building. She lifted her chin. Survive she would! But not if she stayed in Helena, MT.

CHAPTER 2

RICHARD LEWIS SET down the paperwork. "Madam—"

"Don't call me that." Her eyes flashed. "Don't ever call me that again."

"I meant no disrespect, Mrs. Warren."

"Didn't you?"

He hadn't meant to insinuate age. "No, I truly didn't. I wouldn't insult a lady on purpose." It'd be foolish to alienate any client during the economically uncertain times. Lesson one, with this client. Watch his words.

She gave him a direct stare. "All right, then Mrs. Warren is fine." She nodded to the documents on his desk. A tinge of desperation laced her words. "Will you be able to take my case?"

"Yes. I've only skimmed the pages, but I think you have a good chance of proving criminal behavior in court, Mrs. Warren, if we can prove he intended to commit fraud." For the sake of clear communication, Richard asked, "Are there any other words I might offend you with?"

"Are you having sport with me?" She stood and extended her hand to take back the paperwork.

Richard's brow wrinkled. "Sport? Why would I—"

She sized him up a moment, then sat back down. "You mean to say you aren't aware of who I am?"

Besides a very lovely lady with a very touchy vocabulary? "Mrs. Warren, have we met before? It's not a large city, and I haven't been here long, but I don't remember crossing paths with you or your husband."

"No, but most folks know of me."

Know what? He shook his head. She could be the Queen of Sheba as far as he knew. She was definitely as mysterious.

"When did you arrive then?" Mrs. Warren folded her arms and waited.

"I came last June, right before the silver was devalued." This appointment was not going well at a time he really needed new clientele. Quite a few businesses closed their doors and moved on. "I'm sorry to offend you again, ma'am, but I have no idea."

The small upturn on the corner of her mouth fascinated him. But she said nothing. What would she look like with the glow of a full, sunny smile? He tapped the pile between them. "This will wasn't drawn up by my predecessor or myself." Buying a small legal firm might not have been the wisest investment in hindsight. But he had to start somewhere.

"That firm closed their doors and moved to Butte last year along with the accountant." She shook her head. "I've had to rely on Charles' business partner, Mr. Steven Brown, until now."

"Ah, that explains why you sought out new representation." He folded his hands on top of the desk. "Why did you trust him?"

"I had no reason to distrust him. My husband and he had been partners for several years."

"Why do you think this Steven Brown took advantage of you?"

She searched his face. "You might as well hear it from me first if you're going to represent me." Her features stiffened, as did her back. "I met my husband while working at The Coliseum Theatre." She gave him that direct look again, as if she challenged him.

Richard kept his voice as level as possible. "I see." A bordello. She appeared so proper, a young widow who had only recently come out of mourning. But the brunette beauty in the chair across from him had been a—

"Give me my papers please."

"Are you firing me before we start?" Lesson two.

No extended pauses, shocked or not. This lady could read people well.

"You're willing to help me?"

"Of course." Richard tipped his head. How to say it? "You've been wronged, Mrs. Warren. If you'll let me, I intend to do my best efforts to right that wrong."

She pursed her lips and looked out the open window behind him while deciding. Those big brown eyes filled with luminous light, as if God hung a star in each. "All right then."

He swallowed to bring his mind back to the subject. "Mrs. Warren, tell me how you discovered this contract was incorrect to your agreement?"

"I attempted to draw funds to pay my bills this morning." She swallowed. "The clerk warned me my funds were getting low. My husband's partner had withdrawn a substantial sum without my knowledge."

"He's on your account?"

"Yes. According to the clerk, I gave him access with this contract last month. But Mr. Brown's ability to withdraw funds was never discussed, nor would I have done that."

Richard licked a finger and thumbed through the many pages until he found a small sentence granting access to the bank account. "Mrs. Warren, what did you think this contract meant?"

"I thought it gave permission to my husband's partner to work my half of the mine and to hire men for me. He was to act as a foreman, then deposit gold from the mine into the account."

Richard nodded as he checked her interpretation with the document. "So you didn't read this line?" He turned the page around and pointed at the center of page nine.

"Never did we discuss Mr. Brown's ability to withdraw from my account."

"But it's here. You didn't see it?"

She breathed in slowly as she directed her attention to the words. Then, slowly, she raised her gaze to meet his. "No."

He flipped a few pages back in the packet. "I don't see where you signed." He slid the pages apart. The only thing on the last page was a poorly formed capital "E".

"I made my mark."

Richard's head snapped up from the document. "Please don't be offended, but I need to ask if you know how to read and write?"

With a tight expression, she switched her gloves into her left hand. "No, Mr. Lewis, I do not. If you must know, I never passed the third grade." Her hands fidgeted with the fingers on the gloves. "But I am working on it. Teaching oneself reading and writing is not the easiest thing to do."

He nodded. A protective instinct rose within Richard. "Then I'll be sure to read anything you need out loud and answer any questions you have. I want you to understand everything and base your decisions on full knowledge."

"I would appreciate that." She sat back in the chair. "Go ahead. I have time."

"I hadn't planned—"

She raised a brow.

Rule three—expect the unexpected. Clearly, Mrs. Warren meant to hear all ten pages now. His next appointment wasn't for a few hours yet, since clients were dwindling. Why not? "I'll order some coffee and rolls, then we'll start." He put a note in the dumbwaiter.

A short time later, the grocer's wife responded by sending up a pot. They had an arrangement. The grocer carried a monthly tab. Coffee could be ordered, added to the tab, and Mrs. Bach would deliver it for an extra penny per request via the dumbwaiter. Well worth avoiding three stories of stairs balancing a tray of slippery dishes—or for clients that stayed through lunch.

Richard finished reading the last page. He sorted them back into consecutive order and tapped them on the desk to straighten the stack. "I'll need a few days to research with the bank and the county clerk. Would that be acceptable?"

"Yes." As she stood, she held out a hand. "Thank you, both for reading the contract to me and for coffee." Then she gifted him with a genuine smile that reached those big, brown eyes.

Eyes that intrigued him. He stood, mesmerized,

and took her soft hand in his. Her handshake wasn't regal or limp or rough. She made her agreement with confidence, though she didn't allow the touch to linger.

"Mrs. Warren, everyone deserves for their rights to be protected. I intend to stop your account from being plundered."

She seemed more relaxed than when she'd arrived, almost at ease. "When should we meet again?"

"This time next week? That will give me time to research the claim filing and bank policies."

"Yes, I'll look forward to what you find out."

He saw her to the door. Would he earn another smile when they next met?

CHAPTER 3

THE NEWSPAPER SHOULD BE HERE. "LETTIE?" Emmalee called for her housekeeper as she reached the bottom of the grand staircase. She hadn't known the woman long before marrying Charles. They'd hired her right out of the Coliseum Theatre the day Charles came to collect his bride.

As a housekeeper, Lettie didn't have the baggage of a rental lease anymore. She wanted a way out of the dismal life that had already killed her friend — morphine overdose. Take it and sleep away the pain. Take a little more, sleep it away forever.

Emmalee had contemplated it herself. More than once. Held it in her hand the night she met Charles. He'd promised to pay off her lease one day. A lease that allowed for a soiled dove's rent to continually inflate. She had a choice — marriage or stay locked into a life Emmalee couldn't leave unless her debt was paid. And, that meant taking more customers. Then the rent rose again. The system so rigged the cycle became a frenzy of impossibilities. Even if she'd known how to read, what could she do? Running meant being hunted down and brought back. Then those costs would be added on top of the exorbitant lease.

Then one day he did. Charles showed up with money in hand and made good on his promise. Love didn't factor into the deal for Emmalee. One man versus hundreds? There really wasn't any decision to make. He was such a shy, nice man. They didn't have long together, but her affection had grown into a sweet companionship. Companionship. She shivered at her lonliness.

"Lettie, do you have the news?" She called again. Relief at the sight of another person, one who didn't judge her for her past, flooded Emmalee with calm.

"Yes, Mrs. Warren. I've put the paper and a package at the table with your breakfast." Lettie bobbed a curtsy. "I'll get the coffee."

"You're good to me."

"No ma'am. You're good to me. I didn't think you'd keep me after..." Her words trailed off. She dipped her head and made the sign of a cross. "He was one of the good uns."

"I couldn't let you go." She patted her friend's shoulder. They both missed him. But Charles couldn't help them now, rest his soul. Emmalee had some learning to do. "About that coffee."

"I'll bring it in."

"Thank you, Lettie." Though the breakfast eggs and salty sausages smelled delicious, the package held her curiosity. She followed the aroma into the breakfast nook. She hadn't used the dining table since Charles passed. Enough money and all the food she could eat didn't take away the sense of emptiness at a table meant for twelve. One setting graced Emmalee's place. "Did you already eat?"

"Yes, ma'am. I've some shopping to do for dinner."

Emmalee tugged the twine ribbon on the box. "Well, let's be a little careful with the funds. Seems the effects of the silver crash may not be over yet." No need to scare Lettie. If the situation continued, how would she pay for her housekeeper, carriage driver, and groundskeeper? The men would likely find other employment. They had families to provide for, but Lettie was already at the end of her earning ability as a working girl. Her age and the hardships of that life had closed the door to reentry. Neither woman desired that option anyway. Of course, having a housekeeper with a tainted past didn't help Emmalee's social opportunities either. The ladies of the city hadn't accepted or offered an invitation to tea. None of those oh-so-perfect families would want a past prostitute as a housekeeper either. The friend-ship between Emmalee and Lettie grew stronger instead. Both understood the box they lived inside. A safe, but battered box if Emmalee could manage to keep it.

Slipping the brown paper off, she let it fall to the starched linen tablecloth. Then moving the flaps aside, she peered in and recognized the precious gift. Two books that held both mystery and freedom nestled inside. One, a thick school tome. Though she didn't know how it worked, the elusive eloquence of the English language slept in its pages waiting to wake imagination. The other, a Bible. How long would it be before she could discover what it said? Did she want to? Wasn't the holiness of this special book exactly what condemned her?

Lettie set a cup of steaming black coffee beside Emmalee's cooling plate. "Did you order those for your studies?"

"No. Didn't they have a sending address?" She'd seen books like these before. The last teacher she'd known had them on her desk. The occasional preacher had one when he laid a girl to rest.

"Not that I seen."

The preacher that spoke over Charles' grave read a poem from the Bible that sounded so pretty and peaceful. Yea, though I walk through death or something. He made the words sound comforting, like when Charles read to her in the evenings from the newspaper. The timbre of his voice plucked her heartstrings. She couldn't bring herself to stop the paper's daily subscription. Sometimes Emmalee could glean information from the drawings. But the gibberish words meant next to nothing.

Picking up the Bible, Emmalee flipped the first

few delicate pages. "It's beautiful. I've never owned my own books before." She stopped on a page and tried to read the handwriting on it. "Can you read that, Lettie? Long words aren't my strong suit."

"It says to Mrs. E. Warren presented by Richard Lewis."

"That's all?"

"That's an expensive gift. Ain't that enough?"

"Oh. Yes, of course." Emmalee wrinkled her brow as she turned more pages. The writing so tiny the words blurred together as if one unending list of letters. "But he knows I can't read. I wonder why he sent this?"

Lettie shrugged. "Who can know what a man wants except to satisfy himself."

Emmalee looked at her housekeeper and friend. "But a Bible?"

She shrugged again. "What's the other book in the box?"

Reaching in, Emmalee drew out the big volume. "I think it's a school book that tells you what words mean. I can't remember what my teacher called it though."

Lettie pointed to the title. "That word says it's a dictionary,"

"Dictionary. Yes, that sounds familiar." She opened the cover to find more handwriting on the first page. "Lettie, this looks like more than just names."

"It says, '*Mrs. Warren, may your quest for knowledge be*

blessed and your reading skills strengthen by the day. Sincerely, Richard Lewis.'"

"It says all that?" She didn't really want an answer. Emmalee had learned her alphabet in first grade. In second grade, she'd learned a few small words when she could attend, but still couldn't write her own name. Attendance determined by whether a school was close to wherever they lived while Papa chased jobs laying track for the railroad. Then the first week of third grade her mother died of a woman-problem. Schooling ended, rather the attempt did. Her father needed his oldest to mind the two little ones so he could work.

Papa moved them out to Montana chasing the dream of silver, gold, and land. One day he never came home to the one room cabin. Emmalee turned fifteen a few days later. Papa still hadn't returned after a month. She knew. He wasn't coming back.

With winter coming and two siblings, she couldn't provide enough taking in washing from the shrinking mining town. The nuns at the mission promised to care for them, but she was too old for the already full orphan home. At ten and eight, Jesse and Paulina, would be safe while Emmalee sought survival. Walking away as they called after her was the hardest thing she'd ever done.

Following the work, Emmalee found herself farther and farther from her brother and sister. Even if the little ones learned how to read and write like the nuns promised, they'd have no way to find her.

Just as well. She didn't want to see the rejection on their faces or the judgment in their eyes. She couldn't survive that. Anything else, but not that.

"I met a lady at the church this last Sunday. She told me she taught school before taking in all those newsie boys when she hitched up with a miner."

Why Lettie felt it necessary to go inside a church made no sense to Emmalee. "She talked to you?" Lettie usually received worse treatment from those hoity-toity, upright citizens than Emmalee.

"Made me feel real nice, too." Lettie picked up the box, paper, and twine. "She said her and a friend done taught all them boys to read and to have manners." Laughing, Lettie shook her head. "You shoulda seen it. She got eleven boys sittin' in two rows clean across the church building cuz they take up too much space. But they do look like a mama duck trailing her ducklings when they come in an' out."

The picture of a long line of boys in starched white shirts waddling into wooden pews after their mama duck tickled Emmalee. She chuckled with Lettie. "That would be something to see."

"But then they share passin' that little girl one-after-t'other keepin' her happy while the preacher goes 'bout his bizness."

"Boys keeping a little girl happy?"

"Didja ever hear of such?" Lettie nodded with wide eyes. "They dote on the little queenie as much as her daddy does."

"I can't imagine." Surely Lettie exaggerated. Though a weathered woman, she didn't lie.

"Come with me tomorrow."

"I don't know how you find the courage to walk in there." Emmalee brushed her fingers over the Bible's gold-edged pages. "I think the place would burst into flames if we both walked in. At least all those tongues would set to wagging."

"I been talked to by more than just Mizz Russell and her brood."

Emmalee's eyes widened this time. "You have?"

"I been thinkin' ta ask you. But you been so set against it I didn't have the heart to stress you more since you lost your mister."

"Those people," Emmalee swallowed. "They do know what we are?"

"They do know what we been. But who we are is not what we done, says Mizz Russell and her friend Mizz Shanahan."

Emmalee bit the inside of her lip as she thought through all she'd done and recoiled at the reflection. "That doesn't make sense, Lettie. What we do makes us who we are."

"Nope, this preacher's been talking about how we get a second chance. We get to be new."

"I've had my second chance." She raised her hands gesturing at the lovely home they stood in. Three stories, polished wood everywhere, and prettier furniture than either of the brothel sitting rooms displayed. The whole house, not just the downstairs public rooms, all beautifully decorated as a gift for her. "I don't know how long it will last, but I'm grateful for it while we have a time here."

"What if Mizz Russell could help you learn to read? Would you go to at least meet her?"

"You tried." Crinkling her brow, Emmalee glanced at the thick books sitting on her breakfast table. "I think I'm hopeless."

"But I ain't no teacher. I got through sixth grade. But that ain't no help tryin' to teach someone how to do it."

"Why would a stranger help me?"

"She's a teacher. She and Mizz Shanahan done taught them street kids to read, write, and do numbers. The way I hear tell it, them boys was a hootin' up a storm 'fore Mizz Russell got hold of 'em."

Sounding out letters wouldn't help her read books as big as that or the legal documents that said a different number than she'd expected. She needed more than reading skills. Both their futures depended on understanding what she read before it was too late.

"I'll try once. Just to meet this teacher you're going on about."

Lettie's rough face burst into sunshine. "That's fine with me. Yes, just fine."

CHAPTER 4

RICHARD SAT near the middle of the sanctuary. Even there, the loud whispering a few rows behind him caught his notice.

"Now we stand." A snippet caught up to him.

"Why?"

"Just do."

"I feel like I'm riding a trot."

Richard tried not to laugh at the comment as he angled his head to hear her a little better. Going to Sunday meetings could build a person's riding legs, he couldn't argue with that logic. The female voice struck a familiar chord, but he couldn't quite make out the rest of the conversation to place her. It sounded like another woman intended to give instructions throughout the entire service. He'd keep his face forward—and not laugh. He heard the visi-

tor's whisper as they stood for the Gospel,
"Again?"—Richard pretended to cough to cover an
unexpected chuckle. If a new person came for the
first time, they might need a little help from whoever
brought a friend. The last thing they needed would
be undo attention. He'd be sure to welcome the
guest after service though.

Once the service ended, Richard searched the
familiar faces for a newcomer. Then as the Russell
family opened ranks, he saw her. The lovely whis-
perer, and self-proclaimed horsewoman, Mrs.
Emmalee Warren. Was it really her first time in a
church? He walked down the aisle shaking hands
with other members while keeping his new client
within view.

"Good morning, Mr. Lewis." A tad bit of surprise
added a breathy element to her words. "I want to
thank you for such a beautiful gift yesterday."

He lifted her fingers in an acceptable greeting for
a second meeting.

She raised her chin and looked him straight on.
Not challenging, but candid.

"The Bible I sent over must have had a profound
influence to bring you so quickly into the fold."
Would she appreciate his light humor? Or would he
be learning rule number four?

Her eyes lit up and then flicked a glance down-
ward as her lips turned upward. "As a matter of fact,
Mr. Lewis, my purpose here is somewhat influenced
by your thoughtfulness."

"How so, if I may ask?"

"Your gift spurred an idea to find a tutor." She lowered her voice and leaned in to speak quietly. "Mrs. Russell and Mrs. Shanahan have agreed to help me improve my reading abilities, thanks to Lettie's introduction. I'll be able to progress much faster than on my own."

The smaller, older woman heard her name. "Do you need me, ma'am?"

"Always, dear friend." Her face filled with softness. Then she turned back to him. "This dear lady is my housekeeper and friend, Lettie Duncan. She attends here regularly."

She came with her housekeeper? He hadn't noticed the older woman at church before. "Miss Duncan, it's a pleasure." He reached for her fingers to welcome her as he had Mrs. Warren. "A shame we hadn't met sooner."

She pulled her hand back quickly as if uncomfortable with a man's touch. "I sit in back and go right away. Mrs. Warren needs me to get her lunch."

"Well, I'm glad to know you now." He looked between the women. Unusual for an employer to reference a housekeeper as friend. Then again, his new client couldn't be classified as usual. Did Lettie Duncan come out of the brothels as well? She appeared a little rough. He couldn't think of a kinder thing to do than help a woman out of that life and give her a legitimate occupation. "Both of you."

She nodded, a sweet expression on her heavily

pockmarked and lined face. "I'll go call the driver, ma'am."

Mirielle Russell finished her conversation with Calista Shanahan. "Mr. Lewis, good to see you. I'm afraid we have a few hungry tummies to fill." She touched Mrs. Warren's arm. "I'll see you Tuesday? Calista and I will share tutoring for you ladies. That way you'll have lessons twice a week. We'll create a plan with lessons. You'll progress quickly."

Mrs. Warren's expression revealed excitement and determination. "I'm looking forward to it."

The toddler on Mirielle's hip bounced and her hand shot out grasping the brooch on Mrs. Warren's blouse. "Pree—."

Mrs. Warren's hand gently covered the little fingers to prevent a ripping yank. "Yes, pretty." Her eyes misted a moment then cleared. Had that been his imagination? She must miss her husband deeply.

"Janet, no." Mirielle helped disentangle the hold her daughter had on the bauble. "Look, don't touch." She sighed. "New word, you understand."

"Thank you, Janet." Mrs. Warren spoke to the pouting tot who had buried her head in Mirielle's neck. "Lettie says she can't wait to play with the baby."

"That will be a big help while we get our work done to catch you up to her level." She offered a smile in parting to the group as her toddler patted her cheeks chanting, "Pree, Mama."

"Off we go, pretty Janet." She began to gather her boys. "Evan, ready?" Her husband nodded and shook hands with the pastor. "Frankie, round up your brothers." In a flash all the boys filed in behind her as Mr. Russell joined them.

"Well, I'll be." A mystical quirk of her mouth and then she chuckled.

"Mrs. Warren?"

"It is like a little row of ducks, isn't it?"

Richard couldn't keep the laugh to himself. "An excellent observation."

The once crowded sanctuary thinned to a few stragglers leaving Richard with the fascinating Mrs. Warren.

"I do believe your books are about to be well used."

"This is good news."

"Mr. Lewis, may I ask a favor?"

"Anything, if it's within my power."

"If it wouldn't be much trouble, would you consider giving me a list of words from the contract? I can use that list to learn both the definition and spelling." She took a breath. "In the future, I'd like to be able to read and understand words that affect my life."

"Certainly." His admiration grew. Her future would not be ruled by remaining illiterate and he'd do everything possible to help. "It'd be my honor. I'll have it ready at our next appointment."

Light danced in her eyes. "I'm so looking forward to when we next meet, Mr. Lewis."

He cleared his throat. "As do I."

CHAPTER 5

EMMALEE SCRUNCHED her nose and squinted at the words on the page of the Helena Independent. The sketch of several flowers filled the top half. She loved searching the paper to find the list of words Mirielle gave her. It'd become a game. Emmalee loved winning it. When they next met, Emmalee would show her tutor she'd found all the small words in her daily delivery and practiced writing them. The sooner she learned to read and write, the sooner she could sell her house and start over somewhere no one knew either Lettie or Miss Emmie.

"What's all them flowers about?" Lettie poured two cups of coffee and sat in the chair next to Emmalee. The unused dining room worked well for a private classroom.

"I'm not quite sure. I've picked out all the three letter words. I can read and write all of them plus a

few words from my list like state, vote, and club."
She pushed the paper over so Lettie could get a
better look at it. "Can you make sense of it?"

"It says Montana is gonna vote on a state flower."
She whistled. "There's a floral club too."

"Really?" Emmalee touched the sketch of the
primrose and then the wild rose. "Do you remember
how good the trail smelled from Missoula to Helena
with these bushes blooming? Everything was so
fresh and clean. The pink were so sweet and the
yellow ones smelled a bit like lemons."

"Yes, I think that was the best part of the trade. A
few blessedly empty days and no work required."
Lettie patted Emmalee's hand. "A sort of holiday,
wouldn't you say?"

They locked eyes knowing what the other felt and
thought about that nasty business being traded
between brothels. "There's so many pictures in the
paper. Are all the states getting a flower?" Emmalee
held the newspaper up so Lettie could get a better
look. "What else does it say?"

"That line there says Montana has thirty-two bein'
discussed." She pointed at the words. "That's how's
they spell 'thirty-two' with that little line in the
middle and that there's how they spell 'discussed'."
She straightened leaving a hand on the back of
Emmalee's chair. "I seen garden flowers, but I never
did count 'em."

"Thirty-two. No, I didn't know there was that
many in the whole world." Emmalee's curiosity

piqued. "Lettie, I'm going to learn to read this story. Don't read any more."

"Yes, ma'am."

"When are you going to just use my name?" She folded the page down to peer over the top at Lettie. "Charles has been gone a year. You don't have to follow his society rules any longer."

"We're proper now. I'm proud to have a proper occupation and proud that good man of yours done give it to me. Don't you be making me look bad in front of the rest of the housekeepers. I have to shop with those women."

Emmalee laughed. "All right, Lettie." She sobered. "Is it hard to shop for me? Are they very rude?"

"No, not so much. I been judged for bein' a bad woman, I earned that. But I won't be judged for bein' a bad housekeeper. No siree. Don't you be doin' that to me after I worked so hard to get proper."

"Lettie, you're the best woman I know. If that's the way you want it, fine. But couldn't we drop it in the house?"

"That's the way I want it. Good habits and bad habits, we learn 'em both by practice." She crossed her arms. "You just try to get rid of me as your friend, but I ain't breakin' my better habits."

"I'm grateful for you." An excitement filled Emmalee's heart. "Wouldn't being a member of that flower club be fun? I like flowers. I think I like this one best." She pointed to a round, open-faced flower with oblong petals. "It's a happy looking plant, like it's reaching up to the sun and grabbing life."

The bell at the door jangled. "I bet that's our Mizz Russell. Can't wait to set that little cherub she got. I'm goin' to set her to playin' in the kitchen. Them little ones love helpin'." Lettie scooted as fast as her feet could go without running.

"I can't wait to see how this vote turns out. That will be the reward, won't it?" She called after her friend as she noticed line drawings of wild roses, a stalk of iris, and the simple flower with its wide, open face whose name she had yet to learn. "To be able to read without asking for help." She whispered to herself.

Emmalee leaned in to study the drawing. It could be a sunflower, but the seeds were missing. She examined the petals. Maybe a daisy of some sort. They grew everywhere like weeds. The only flower names she could read were rose, lily, and iris. Each four letters. She could sound them out. Then again, each had been the name of a girl she knew in the past.

"Good afternoon." Mirielle met Emmalee with a light hug. "Look at what you've done since we last met."

Two sessions down, the third about to start. The dining room table boasted pages and pages of written and memorized words. Written on both sides and stacked neatly, evidence that Emmalee spent her free time in education, also that she needed more paper.

"I think it's time we put some of these words into short sentences. Shall we?"

"I'd be delighted." Emmalee drew her newest friend's attention to the Helena Independent. "Do you, by chance, think I could read this one article anytime soon?"

"Sooner than you think, Emmalee." She slipped into the chair Lettie had vacated and picked up the much-marked article sporting circles around all the words from Emmalee's last lesson. Mirielle looked over the page and then asked, "Are you interested in any social activities?"

Emmalee bit her lip. Yes! Yes, she wanted social activities. Not that it should matter since she'd be leaving soon. Then there was the problem of fitting in. "I'm not so sure."

"What do you think of joining the Montana Floral Emblem Association? We're always looking for new members."

"I don't think they'd want me there. I'm surprised you don't seem to mind visiting with me." She stopped suddenly. "Or, don't you know about me?"

Mirielle put the paper down. "I do. You are a wonderful person worth knowing. Anyone would be blessed to know you."

"I'm blessed you think so." Emmalee clasped her hands. "But very few others feel the same way. I can see it in their eyes when they look at me—and when some won't."

"Then let's change that, shall we?"

"I haven't been able so far." Emmalee took the article and set it aside. "I couldn't begin to know how."

"People need to get to know you. Come to the floral association with me. I'd love to introduce you to my friends." Mirielle turned in her chair. "The best way through a wall is to walk through a door. I would like to be that doorway for you."

Emmalee walked into the church with a friend. The people there welcomed them. Maybe she could walk into the Montana Floral Emblem Association with another. Leaving Helena on good terms with at least a few people would feel less a failure. Maybe she wouldn't have to lie to start over. Maybe it'd be less like running away and more like a wise financial decision.

"I promise not to leave you on your own."

She gave one dip of her chin. "I'll think on it. But I'd prefer to know how to read before I go into a crowd. At the church, I can sing along and say the prayers because I hear the others. I have a good ear." Laying a hand on the article, Emmalee added, "I don't know what goes on in a place like that. What if I have to read something?"

"No one has to read publicly. We can read anything they hand out at the meetings during our lessons." Mirielle's voice took on a passion. "Imagine women voting. It may be a flower, but it's going to be our state flower. We're setting a precedent for future generations."

"Women having a say about the future?"

"There's talk of taking a vote by September. We need your vote, Emmalee. Can I count on you to help us?"

Not a demand. A question. A question that left the decision up to her whether she wanted to take part. "I'll go."

"Well then, I see a bright future for you." She handed a piece of paper and a pen to Emmalee. "In order to vote, you'll need to have a signature."

RICHARD WATCHED THE CLOCK TICK THEN tock. The morning passed slower than it took a caterpillar to crawl a limb. Meeting Emmalee Warren changed how Richard tracked time. He didn't used to watch the clock hands and urge them to speed up. Finally, his Seth Thomas clock struck eleven. As the last deep baritone chime echoed in his office, the knock on the door's glass inset sped up his heart. She'd come. The news he had to deliver wasn't going to be good. However, the judge wouldn't like it either and that was very good.

He opened the door and ushered in his favorite client. "How are you this lovely morning, Mrs. Warren?" Richard slid a chair out from his desk to seat her in the smallish office.

"Well thank you, and you?" She accepted and sat, shifting her light green skirts to the side so Richard could step past to his desk. Pale green suited her coloring, a little pink from the exertion of climbing three stories on a hot summer day. The matching sunhat she wore tipped forward, angled across her forehead. Pink, green, and white ribbons curled around the brim rolling into little decorative flowers with white feather down tucked in amongst them. Ash brown tendrils escaped her elegantly rolled hair. She set a black leather valise and her parasol beside her on the floor.

"Quite well. First, your request." He handed over a sheet of paper. "I made a list of the words I thought would be most helpful to you."

"I'm sure they will, Mr. Lewis." She smiled as she glanced it over then slid the page into the valise. I very much appreciate your thoughtfulness."

He liked being the cause of that smile. "Richard, please."

She searched his face a moment. "Emmalee."

"Emmalee." He'd managed to move them from stiff formality to acquaintance, a step toward trust. If she didn't hate the messenger by the end of their meeting. " As to your case, we have a number of items to discuss. I've found cause to petition the court to review the documents."

"What did you find?"

"This document," he held it up, "you brought me is legal, but the manner of obtaining your mark involved misrepresentation. The first part of our petition will need to prove that beyond doubt for the court." He'd start from the beginning and build their case, then show continued unlawful actions gaining severity. "I also discovered the remaining employees knew the original mine petered out."

"That man told me it was producing well. I can abide many things, but not a liar and a cheat." She stood as if propelled by righteous anger, and Richard stood with her.

"We'll need to prove you were duped into continuing to invest."

She jammed her fists onto her slim hips targeting Richard in her frustration. "I'm not stupid, you know. I understand what needs to happen to keep a mine operating."

Lesson three. Illiterate doesn't mean uneducated in the ways of the world. He held up a hand. "Not once did I entertain the thought that you were less than a competent and intelligent woman. Mr. Brown used your inability to read to commit fraud."

Emmalee began pacing the narrow aisle from wall to wall, arms crossed. "He's coming tomorrow at four."

Tomorrow. That piece of information changed things drastically. "How often do you have to meet with Mr. Brown?" A warm breeze blew through the window. Air movement helped as the day continued to warm. Noise from the carriages in the street below filtered in through the third story window as well.

"The beginning of each month to sign for my share of supplies, wages, and get a report on the production of both mines."

Richard rubbed his hand across the back of his neck easing the stiff collar. Monthly. How many more documents did he need to chase down and search for a line or two whittling away at the pretty widow's estate? "Don't sign anything. Delay a few days to let me finish putting all the pieces in place. Then we'll bring in the sheriff to arrest Mr. Brown." He slowly turned keeping in time with whichever direction she paced, his body language open.

She thought for a moment. "I've never missed a meeting. He'll know something's wrong. I've always signed after he tells me everything. Well, his version of everything." She shook her head and resumed circling his office like a wild horse in a pen. "Charles believed in him and I believed in Charles."

"I fear that may have been a serious mistake. Emmalee, sometimes loving someone can blind us to the facts."

"Love did not blind me. I cared for my husband and I miss him. But I don't believe in love, Mr. Lewis."

"I see."

"And you think that's horrible, don't you?"

Lesson four. Don't assume.

"Not at all. Please forgive my presumptions."

She looked at him and then nodded, but resumed her pacing.

"Emmalee, we need to discuss another problem." Richard moved forward and caught her hand to halt her. "I've discovered your share of the mining claim has been registered as sold to Mr. Brown in exchange for his rights on the original mine." He let her go in case she needed to pace away the nerves.

"What?" Astonishment paled her cheeks then she rallied. "Why didn't you tell me that right away?"

Lesson five. Don't try to soften the blow. "There's more. Please take a seat."

Emmalee didn't budge a step. The heat of the day or anger streaked red up from the high white lace neckline to the roots of her comely coif. The loose tendrils danced around her neck distracting Richard. Stay on track, man. Besides that this woman came to him as a client, he didn't want to create any further distrust. He needed to keep his growing attraction under control. He blinked and looked away though a light scent of rose water wafted his direction.

"What can be worse than losing the source of my income completely?"

Richard took a deep breath before delivering the rest of his devastating news. "I found out from the court clerk that Mr. Brown has drawn up a change of ownership deed for your home. He bragged that the deed would be registered by the end of the week."

"He can't do that!"

"Evidently Mr. Brown has gained confidence from his past escapades."

"He's going to come tomorrow and take my house." Wide-eyed as she said the words, she winced at the next realization. "Besides myself, I have Lettie to think about." Emmalee put her hands on her cheeks. "He's going to steal my house, too!"

Richard laid his other hand on top of hers to add encouragement to his words. "Not if you don't sign, he can't."

"Well I didn't sign anything saying he could take over my half of the working mine either, that's for certain, and he managed to do it anyway!"

"You meet with him every month. Do you sign anything during those meetings?"

"Just the reports."

"Does anyone else read the reports before you do for legal or business purposes?"

Mrs. Warren shook, trembled like an avalanche until she dropped off the cliff of disbelief. "No." She whispered as she slowly sat in the chair and slipped her hand from his. "He reads the reports to me. I make my mark. When he takes the gold into the bank, the clerk knows to deposit half in Mr. Brown's account and half in mine."

"Did you get statements after the deposits?" Not wanting to crowd her or hover, Richard moved back and leaned against the desk. He stayed close in case she fainted from the stress.

The saddest eyes he'd ever seen stared up at him

in a face as white and stiff as marble. "He's been fleecing me this whole time, hasn't he?" Her eyes brightened with unshed tears, but underneath an exciting fierceness coiled.

"If he'd been gaining confidence by taking a little, then a little more, this latest act may be for the only thing you have left."

"I need that home so I can sell it to start over somewhere else."

Wait—start over? "Are you planning on going somewhere?"

"What does that matter if I have nothing left?" She rolled her lips inward as if staving off a scream. "I don't know what I'll do now." Tears shimmered on her cheeks as she whispered, "Please help me. I know I'm not worth your trouble, but I don't want to go back to that life." Droplets fell freely. "Lettie can't go back. She'd never survive it even if she could find a place that would take her."

"I will help you because you are worth helping." Richard knelt on one knee beside her. "God's keeping a record of all your tears." He tugged a handkerchief out of the breast pocket and tucked it into her palm. "If God thinks enough to count your individual tears and record them in his book, then he finds you invaluable, Emmalee—and so do I."

She whispered as she dabbed away the salty streaks, "I think counting my tears are a waste of his time and yours. If there's a god, he has a lot more to do than think one whit about me. If he did care, he'd have shown up a long time ago."

"Nothing about you is a waste of the Almighty's time. You know how I can prove it?"

Handing Richard back the hanky, she waited for his answer.

"Because you're not a waste of my time. I consider you a very important client." He held her gaze with his. "Let me help you."

"How? Do you hold a trump card?" The distrust played across her features. "I have to meet that man and he's going to have that deed. What's he going to do when I don't sign?"

"Don't meet Steven Brown alone, Mrs. Warren. As your attorney, and I hope your new friend, I advise you to bring your meetings to my office."

"Then he'll know he's been caught and just run off before he ever shows." She pushed back in her chair, away from Richard. "I sign and I lose all I have left. I don't do it, and meet him here, he runs off with all he's stolen or worse." She shook her head. "Who's going to care whether a whore get justice?"

"I do." He looked her straight in the eyes. "And you're not a whore. God doesn't see you that way and neither do I. You're a widow who deserves to be protected, that's in the Gospel. We're instructed to watch over widows and orphans." She hadn't outright rejected the offer of friendship. "Brown's not aware you know what he's been up to or that you're learning to read and write. We can use that to get evidence." He cocked his head as an idea struck. "What if you managed to get a hold of the documents he brings tomorrow and get interrupted before you sign?"

She lifted a hand to swipe tickling hair away from her nose. "I see. Make it impossible to get business done and reschedule to be polite."

"What if you had a few nosey ladies stop in tomorrow at, say, four in the afternoon? Wouldn't it be a shame if they wouldn't take no for an answer?"

Two small indents formed at the bridge of her nose. "Where am I going to find women willing to visit me?"

He grinned. "I have it on good authority that the church sends the hospitality committee to welcome guests that attended services. May I have your permission to schedule a committee visit? You might want to ask Lettie to have a little tea and cookies prepared. I've heard the ladies do enjoy a nice, long chat."

"It would be my first opportunity to entertain." She looked almost terrified. "No one has ever accepted before. What if I can't—"

"Mrs. Emmalee Warren, you are a lovely woman with a sweet personality. Not only are you going to be a successful hostess, but we're going to gain the evidence and time we need to prepare our offense." If he could win this case, maybe she would stay in Helena. A client's choice to stay or go shouldn't matter to him. But it did. How would she react to the last piece of the puzzle? "Did you know your husband registered a large nugget from a new claim the day before he died?

"No."

If she didn't already suspect foul play, he may have a hysterical female on his hands in a moment. Though Mrs. Emmalee Warren seemed more the type to meet the issue square on, anyone would crack under this mother lode of betrayal. "His partner knew. Both signatures are on the claim deposit." Richard kept his voice steady and calm. "That nugget has already been sold, according to the filing office. Unfortunately, without you present, the bank cannot tell me if there's been a deposit to your account and won't tell me anything about Mr. Brown's. Will you go to the bank with me in the morning?"

Her eyes closed and she gave a small shake of her head. "That was last year, Mr. Lewis."

"Richard." He reinforced. Would she trust him after what men like Steven Brown had done to her? Could she trust anyone after the life she'd led?

"What good would that do us now if that man has spent the money?"

"If the amount of the nugget's worth and the amount your partner withdrew match from yours or deposited to his, then we have the beginnings of proof. You can press charges and file for reparation."

She glanced at his face and nodded. "Richard. Are you sure about the date they found the nugget?"

"Yes."

Emmalee ducked her head and covered her face with her hands. A quiet, muffled question snuck into the air. "What if it wasn't a mine collapse at all?"

There. The question he'd been wondering since uncovering this mishmash about a missing gold nugget. "Then our case moves from claim jumping and fraud to murder."

"My husband was a good man. I may not have been in love with him, but I deeply respected and cared about him." She stood, all shaking and shock gone. "How do we catch this criminal?"

"I'll make an appointment for us first thing tomorrow morning to meet with the bank president, Mr. Thomas Marlow. I feel certain, once he hears your story, that he'll help us."

She nodded. Then a calm smile touched her lips. "Where did you hear of such a thing as God counting and recording tears? It's—a pretty sentiment."

"It's not just a story I made up, Emmalee. You'll enjoy the Psalms as your reading progresses."

"That's a book, then?"

He smiled. "It's in the Bible I sent you."

She tipped her head to the side as she spent a moment looking closely at his face. "All right, I'll start working on those Psalms. They seem to have some nice words."

"I find them very comforting in many situations. The Psalms are God's way of telling me he understands our human emotions since he created them."

"Well I certainly hope there's one about how I feel right now." She gave him a wry side-glance. "But I don't know if God would appreciate what I'm thinking."

"Why don't you try Psalm twenty-five? You might be surprised."

A wisp of a smile crossed her lips. "I'll see you in the morning."

Richard watched her go. For a small office, it seemed awfully empty all of a sudden.

CHAPTER 6

EMMALEE AND RICHARD sat in teakwood chairs
on the rounded side of the massive kidney-shaped
desk in Thomas Marlow's office. Emmalee let
Richard do the talking. The only way she'd ever
communicated with a rich man was with her body.
She'd never met this rich man at the Coliseum
Theatre.

"You're sure the nugget's value matches the
amount in that withdrawal?" Richard asked the First
National Bank and Trust president.

"Absolutely." Mr. Marlow addressed Emmalee,
"You're a lucky woman, Mrs. Warren, to have Richard
Lewis representing you."

"Thank you, sir." She glanced at her lawyer. "He's
been a godsend."

Richard shrugged off the compliment. "I haven't

done anything that any good attorney wouldn't do. But I appreciate your confidence." He added, "What do you think you can do to protect the remaining funds?"

"Based on the documents you've provided, ma'am, I'll draw up a set of statements showing transfers from one account to the other. They seem to have corresponded with the dates on each of the pages here. I'll have them ready to present as evidence for the judge. Get me a court order and I can also freeze both accounts until the judge makes a ruling." He laughed making his thick brown mustache wiggle. "Can't see Mr. Brown hightailing it out of town without the money he's accumulated, can you?"

"That will help." Richard agreed. "But Emmalee, will that cause you undue hardship?"

She gulped. Would she lose her employees if they didn't get paid on time? "Is there any other way around it? People are counting on their pay." She could scratch out an existence, but the others had family and mouths to feed.

Thomas Marlow thought for a moment, his fingers steepled below his clean-shaven chin. "I can open a new account for you. You can transfer the needed funds for the next month until this all sorts out. The new account would not have any letters attached to it allowing anyone but you access. Then we can put a new letter on file right now directing any gold, dust or nuggets, that comes in daily to deposit into your new account."

Emmalee breathed a sigh of relief. Richard's plan might work. At least she wouldn't lose any further funds. "May I have Mr. Lewis draft that for me?"

"Yes, Mrs. Warren, I think that's a wise idea. If you will, Mr. Lewis, I'll witness her signature and we'll put it into action immediately. I'll have you stop with me and see the teller for the account on your way out. I can't promise Mr. Brown won't catch on though." He had a pained expression. "Awful situation. I'd suggest you move quickly with the courts."

"We will, thank you." After he'd drafted the letter Richard handed the fountain pen to Emmalee.

This would be her first official signature. Not a mark, her full flourished name though she'd used a pencil all night. She felt the weight of the fountain pen between her thumb and fingers. A sense of confidence swirled up in her and she signed in a smooth motion—Mrs. Emmalee Louise Warren.

Her triumphant grin left the two men speechless and staring. "I did it right, didn't I?"

Stumbling over one another, they both agreed. "Yes."

"Absolutely." Mr. Marlow nodded. "I, uh… I was under the impression you couldn't read or write, Mrs. Warren."

"I've been receiving tutoring." She felt so proud of her ability she nearly giggled.

Lesson six. Don't underestimate how fast she can learn. Richard found his tongue. "I believe those lessons are paying off, Emmalee." His eyes spoke admiration that tickled something in the pit of her stomach. "Let's be sure that your signature and your mark are recognized as belonging to the same person. Would you mind making your mark beside your signature?"

"Certainly."

"And Mr. Marlow, would you sign here that you've witnessed Mrs. Emmalee Warren as having made both the mark and the signature?"

"It will be my honor." He signed as witness. "Ma'am, you are to be congratulated for your perseverance and quick mind."

How many years had it been since she blushed? Emmalee flushed with pleasure.

Mr. Marlow accompanied Emmalee and Richard to see the teller. He had the new account opened, most of the remaining funds transferred, and directions to deposit any money or gold into it discreetly, handled in no time. With only a few employees, the bank president gave his word no one would let on that anything had changed. The next time Mr. Brown arrived to siphon money into his account, the bank had a plan in place to notify the sheriff and her attorney.

All their business concluded, Richard stuck out his hand at the bank's doorway and shook hands with Thomas Marlow. "I'll be back this afternoon with the court order to freeze the two accounts."

Emmalee also shook hands with the gentleman. "I don't know how to thank you."

"No need, ma'am." He held the door for them to exit. "Good luck."

CHAPTER 7

AT THE SOUND of the electric doorbell, Lettie dropped the spoon sending sugar and cinnamon all over the cutting board. "He's here, Mrs. Warren." She swept a hand across the board dumping the sugar mixture into her apron. Then after a quick shake over the rubbish bin, she clapped the rest off her hands. In her nervous rush, Lettie didn't notice most of the mess landing on the polished wood floor. "Keep calm. Take your time. Remember Mr. Lewis said don't sign nothin' at all."

Emmalee caught her friend's arms and looked into her eyes. " It's going to be all right." She gave Lettie a quick hug. "We're going to be all right. Mr. Lewis has it under control. All you need to do is let everyone in. You're fine now?" She nodded slowly until Lettie nodded with her, eyes locked together.

"Good. Go let that snake in before he gets suspicious."

Lettie smoothed her apron and hustled to the door.

"Mr. Brown, come in. Mrs. Warren is expecting you. I was just in the kitchen making cookies. Let me get her for you and get back to those cookies before they're all black-bottomed."

Emmalee heard it all and quietly closed her eyes, shaking her head. Lettie talked more in those two minutes to that man than she had in two years.

Lettie led Steven Brown into the sitting room, dirty boots and all.

He sat in Charles' brown leather armchair without an invitation or a greeting to Emmalee first. He sniffed the buttery cinnamon aroma coming from the kitchen. "Wouldn't mind a cookie, if ya got one ta spare."

"I'm sure we can spare a cookie or two for a hard-working man like you, Mr. Brown." She kept her face controlled and turned away from his highhanded manners. He preened under Emmalee's skill garnered from years of plying customers with overly sweet compliments. "Lettie, would you mind bringing in a tray of cookies and coffee for Mr. Brown, please? Coffee, yes?" She glanced at him.

"That'd be mighty fine of ya, Miss Emmie."

How many times had she warned him? "Again, Mr. Brown, please do not refer to me as Miss Emmie.

I left that life behind a long time ago. I prefer Mrs. Warren or Emmalee, if you must."

He waved away her complaint. "Whatever ya want. Let's get down ta business."

She gave him a stern glare. "I do want you to respect my wishes, Mr. Brown."

"Sure, sure." He pulled several folded pages out of his pocket. "You need me to read these monthly statements to you or if you don't want to waste time just make yer mark here."

Bold! He'd never asked to skip the fake reading before. "No, we've had a habit. I don't like to change something that's working. Please, by all means read them to me. I'd really like to know how things are going at the mines." She almost laughed at his scowl, but caught herself. "It's important to know what's going on in one's business, don't you think, Mr. Brown?"

He leaned his elbows on his knees as he read. "Says here the original mine is going at normal production. I ain't yet got as high returns outta the new mine, but she's gonna come through for us one day." He looked up with a self-satisfied smirk.

She kept her voice sultry sweet, the kind of purr she used in the past. "I'm sure it will with you over-seeing the operation. Charles would be ever so proud of what's happening here." He would too. Emmalee sent up a good thought to her honest husband. *I know you're smiling down on me, dear. If there's a god up there, would you mind telling him I could use a little help catching this cooncat?*

"I replaced two of them Chinamen that up and left for California a week ago. All the supplies are about the same as last month."

The quarter hour chimed on the cuckoo clock. Shouldn't the church ladies be here by now? Emmalee needed to slow him down. "I don't remember what all those supplies were. Can you remind me please?"

"Aw, we don't need to go over all that, now do we?"

Emmalee looked at the clock. "Yes—"

Lettie carried in a tray loaded with delicate demitasse cups, a plate of warm snickerdoodles, a jar of sugar, and a little pitcher of cream. "Mr. Brown, might you move that side table so I can set this down between you?"

While he turned his back to pick up the small table, Lettie signaled her concern.

Emmalee acknowledged it with a hand motion to move slower, and sent an encouraging smile.

The table settled in place, Lettie moved a snail's pace as if the coffee would spill. Then nearly did spill it when she jumped at the electric doorbell. "Who could that be?" Her tone tinged a bit on the melodramatic side.

Emmalee forced a straight poker face. "Would you mind seeing to that while Mr. Brown continues his reading?"

"Yes, ma'am."

The moment the door opened a dozen ladies poured into the house. Calista Shanahan carried in her wriggling baby boy while a few others tugged along older toddlers including Mirielle and little Janet. A buzz of excitement added both confusion and loud conversation. Neither Emmalee or her business partner could hear one another.

"The church welcoming committee is here to see you, Mrs. Warren!" Lettie announced over the chaos.

She didn't even try to hold back her grin. The ladies' greetings enveloped her in a circle of fun exclamations from happy friends. If only it were real. A wave of want doused Emmalee's heart—until Lettie continued the playacting.

The housekeeper threw her arms in the air and spun on a heel. "I'll bring more cookies."

Emmalee took her cue, intentionally softening her words. "Mr. Brown, I do—"

"What'dja say?"

Were the ladies intentionally raising the noise level? It was getting harder to suppress an outright laugh. She raised her voice a tiny bit, "I said I do believe we're going to need to reschedule."

He grabbed for the papers he'd set down by the cookie tray. "I'll be back tomorrow."

She stepped closer. "No, I'll be gone all day. I'll get someone to finish reading—"

"We gotta get this done." He yelled over the din.

Calista's infant let out a squall scared by a booming male voice.

Emmalee wanted to double over at the baby's participation, however unaware the poor little thing was. "How's Thursday afternoon?"

"But—"

"Mr. Brown, you certainly need to get all this business done for me." She batted her lashes. "But the bank isn't going to be open during the holiday anyway." She patted his arm. "I know how important it is. I'd never want to interfere and cause us both to lose time that's so important. Yes, come Thursday at the end of the day and we'll wrap this up."

He growled, "I'll do that." He began folding the paperwork.

"Why don't you just leave that here with me? I'll get someone to help me read them over and I can have them delivered to you after I si—uh, make my mark."

She read panic in his eyes. "No!" He tightened his grip on them and backed up. "Thursday is fine."

Emmalee couldn't see another way to get hold of the paperwork. Best to let him go. "I'll see you then. Do please take a cookie with you."

He grabbed a handful of the treats and stuffed them in a pocket. They'd be a mass of crumbs before he made it to the corner. Emmalee choked back a laugh. He proved greedy about everything.

The ladies closed ranks and propelled him out the

door. Once it shut behind him, they burst into applause.

When the crowded sitting room quieted, Emmalee held up the tray. "Cookie?"

They all laughed while finding seats. Lettie collected the handful of children scooting them off to their own tea party with a nanny to help her.

"How can I thank you all?"

Calista flicked a hand. "It's nothing. We all are enjoying the intrigue." She reached for a snickerdoodle. "We'd have been here sooner, but you know how that trolley system runs on its own schedule." A murmur of collective resigned agreement scattered around the room.

Mirielle added, "Did you see the look on his face?" Another round of feminine laughter then Mirielle introduced the other ladies. "Emmalee, all of us are here as the church welcoming committee. We want you to know that both you and Lettie are invited to join us each week. We're having a picnic tomorrow to celebrate Independence Day. Zelda's in charge of potluck dishes." She pointed to the quiet woman in the corner chair. "Would you and Lettie come?"

Could it be possible that this circle of women would become her friends? Bemused, she nodded. "I'll ask Lettie." There didn't seem to be a separation between classes with these people. Why?

Mirielle bit into her cookie, chewed, and held it

up. "In fact, I think I speak for all of us when I say we nominate Lettie to bring these cookies! The scent alone is decadent." The agreement around the circle rang nearly as loud as their entrance had been.

"I have you down for snickerdoodles," Zelda said. She didn't seem quite as bubbly as the rest.

"I'll be sure to tell Lettie her recipe is a winner." Good humor and a niggle of belonging wrapped their happy arms around Emmalee. She wanted to snuggle in those arms forever. This was what happiness felt like. Emmalee wouldn't let anything stop her from attending that picnic.

Calista took over. "The next invitation from all of us is to attend the Helena chapter of the Montana Floral Emblem Association. Our next meeting is a new membership drive." Her warm words cinched it for Emmalee. "We're going to learn about each of the thirty-two possible state flowers."

The hour flew, punctuated by the quarterly bird popping out of his nest to cuckoo his annoyance at the summer sun's refusal to set. Emmalee agreed to go to a picnic, the floral club, and church. A year ago, even a month ago, not one of these things had entered her mind. The sense of community involvement tasted better than the buttery crumbs of a snickerdoodle melting on her tongue. She made a mental note to search out community activities in the next town she moved to after the house sale. Without her spoiled reputation, perhaps blending

into society would happen more easily than it had
the two hard years here. And, she'd have had the
practice of these social events under her belt. She'd
be less likely to misstep.

CHAPTER 8

RICHARD WAVED at the last of the ladies leaving
Emmalee's home.

"Will you come in?" Emmalee stood with her
hands behind her back leaning against the door.

"It would be my pleasure." He doffed his hat.
Lettie took it and plunked it on the rack in the foyer.
"Thank you, Lettie. Mm, smells good in here."

Emmalee led him into the sitting room still scattered with extra chairs, lemonade glasses, and cookie
crumbs dashed around the room by cooped up
youngsters. "I'm afraid we're a little tumbled at the
moment."

Richard looked around and back to his hostess.
She seemed full of joy, not bothered at all by the
mess left by so many sudden guests. Lesson seven.
Emmalee cared more about people than things. He
should have quit collecting his list. He knew enough

to represent her well. But this client did something to his insides. He wanted to really know her—Richard's list grew each time they met. For a woman of the evening, she had more virtues than most of the women he'd met. Virtues he admired as much as he admired that elusive, uninhibited smile. "It appears your party was a success."

She nearly glowed as bright as the moon on a dark night. The kind a man can't take his eyes off and that dims all the stars in the sky. "Lettie might have one or two snickerdoodles hidden away for you."

Then without having to call her, Lettie appeared with a little plate holding one cookie and a glass of cool, sweet lemonade. "I made sure to keep this one back for you, Mr. Lewis."

"I must be a lucky man to get the last of your baking. The ladies went on and on out on the stoop." He accepted them from her. "I wondered if I'd get in to actually taste one or if they'd eaten them all." He winked at Emmalee.

"Well you enjoy it, sir." Lettie headed back to the kitchen, but tossed a comment over her shoulder. "I'll make sure you get a dozen from my next batch."

Richard's brows lifted at Emmalee. He drank half the glass as Emmalee told him all about the party.

"We've been volunteered to bring snickerdoodles tomorrow to the big Independence Day picnic. Lettie's right proud of how they went over today." The sound of dishes clunking around in the kitchen punctuated her statement. She leaned forward and whispered, "I think she's started already."

He chewed a large bite, then said, "She should be proud. I think these would win a blue ribbon!" As he finished eating and polished off the drink, he listened to the results of their plan.

"So he did take the papers. I don't know what else I could do. But the crowd you sent over made sure he couldn't cause any more trouble." She outright twinkled with glee. "That poor man couldn't make out heads or tails over the noise."

The inner sparkle shining in Emmalee's eyes nearly caused Richard to forget the line of their conversation. He raised an empty glass and swallowed air. Did she know the effect she had on him? Or was it commonplace for men to flop at her feet?

"More lemonade?"

"Uh, yes." He held the glass out and she poured the last of the pitcher for him. "Too bad we don't have the document, but our ultimate goal was to buy time. While you entertained Mr. Brown and the ladies this afternoon, I did manage to see Judge W. F. Hunt. He agreed your case has merit and issued a court order to freeze the two accounts with a full understanding that we'll be bringing the case to court in front of him in the near future."

"That's wonderful!" She clasped her hands together. "Now what do we do?"

"We continue building evidence and wait for Steven Brown to make his next move." Richard leaned back in the chair. "The sheriff has been notified. If Mr. Brown attempts to withdraw funds or acts in any other illegal manner, we'll have him. I've also been successful in discovering that though the mine deeds were shuffled, Mr. Brown has not yet finalized the dissolution of the partnership."

"I don't understand."

"Meaning, the partnership still holds ownership over both mines. When Mr. Brown is arrested and found guilty, the ownership of the entire operation will revert to you."

Emmalee launched herself off of her chair and hugged Richard. His arms closed around her as naturally as if she belonged to him. That's when he knew. He was falling for a woman who didn't believe in true love. Why would she after all she'd experienced? Just one more man to take a precious part of her. At least he could try getting to know her and see if she'd like to get to know him.

He reluctantly pulled away. Clearing his throat, he said, "Emmalee, would you allow me to accompany you to the upcoming picnic?"

Her happy countenance stayed. "Absolutely, Richard." She seemed a little breathless.

"Then I'll come by with my carriage and drive you to the Broadwater for the festivities. I'll help with the blankets and baskets so you ladies won't have to rustle them on the trolley line." He started for the door. "We'll have a glorious day."

She followed and held the door handle, though hadn't opened it.

"Thank you, Emmalee, for a most pleasant visit." With you, his heart thumped.

"You're always welcome here."

"I'll get back to work now." He gazed at her not moving to leave.

She smiled. "Yes." They stood in the entry smiling into each other's eyes.

Lettie handed over his hat, surprising Richard when it slid between him and Emmalee. "Don't want to forget this."

Where had the housekeeper come from? He blinked. "Well, then, uh…goodbye for now."

Emmalee nodded—with those shining, starry eyes. "Yes. Until then."

Lettie looked between them with a quizzical expression. "Alrighty, you come back now." She took the door handle from her mistress and pulled it open.

"Yes, yes I will." He backed out the door. The hot sun angling toward the mountains warmed his shoulders through the dark suit coat. "See you soon then."

"WHAT WAS YOU TWO ALL GETTING ON about?" Lettie asked.

Emmalee held the curtain aside and watched

Richard disappear around the corner toward the trolley stop. "I don't know."

"That was like watching two little moo cows bop noses for the first time in the pasture." She piled dishes on a tray from the sideboard. "Like neither one's seen another animal like itself before. Next thing ya know and you'll be cavortin' around the field makin' a spectacle."

"I…I really don't know what you mean." Emmalee swished her pink skirt to the side to move into dinner. She'd purposefully worn an understated skirt and white cotton shirtwaist. The plainer the better so as not to appear expecting company. How then, in her plainest outfit, her hair not even in a proper pompadour, did it seem Richard Lewis found her interesting?

"I mean it's not a good idea to go getting' all muddled up if you can't really do anything about it." Her worry for her friend bare on her face. "I don't think you want a dilly-dally this time since you've gone all respectable and such. Do you?" Tray filled, Lettie took it to the kitchen.

Emmalee knew Lettie's advice stemmed from a life of disappointment. She ducked her head. How could she answer what she wanted when she didn't know?

Rounding the hall corner, Lettie came back still sharing her worry and wisdom as if she hadn't left the room. "I'm tellin' you his family won't approve and you'll be hurt. Just one more man takin' what ain't his in the first place. Better we follow your plan and get on our way soon as it's all said and done." Lettie slid chairs back in place as she talked on. "Then you find yerself a decent man where we go. We can't be the mooneye little fools that them other women get to be." She pushed the piano bench back under the upright. "No, ma'am. You've got to think smart or you got no future. And you havin' a future means I have a future too, you know."

Lettie's wisdom shot a sharp bullet of truth regardless of the delivery. Emmalee nodded. "But I've promised to go to the picnic with him. I accepted for you as well."

"I don't think—"

"Lettie, with you along, it'll be a good reminder not stray from our goal." She hugged her friend. "I know you mean best for the both of us. Listen, all the miners seem to be heading to California. I've been thinking to go on to Seattle." She took Lettie's hand and drew her into the dining room. The morning paper lay open on the table with an article well circled. "Or a completely different direction, somewhere in Arizona Territory where copper mines are making rich men who need proper wives." Far enough that Miss Emmie's reputation could be shed.

"You can't just go showin' up. Lone women get the wrong kind of reputation."

"I've thought of that, too." She turned a few of the pages back until she found an entire article circled.

"That's an ad for wives. I'll answer it. You go with me and find a man of your own."

"You won't know what yer gettin'. And me?" She shook her head vehemently. "I ain't got a need to have another man but ever! Nope. Not gonna let one more man touch me." She set her face with iron. "I'll be a proper worker till I can't work no more. Then if the good Lord is as kind as they say, he'll just take me away."

"Then if I pay my own way, I don't have to take him either. I won't owe anybody anything."

"I'll go with you like we planned then. But don't be getting' any ideas of hitching me off to some hooligan."

Emmalee grinned. "I won't. I'll be selfish and keep you with me."

Lettie grinned back. "We have an agreement." She turned on her heel and left. A moment later she returned with a broom and dustpan. In short work she had the room cleaned as if a party had been a figment of imagination.

Emmalee hugged her arms around her waist. But it wasn't imaginary. She hummed walking up the stairs. At least two or three of the ladies might really be friends. Pausing with a hand on the gleaming hardwood rail, Emmalee realized she'd have a hard time saying goodbye to them.

CHAPTER 9

EMMALEE HELPED LETTIE PACK fried chicken, freshly picked berries from the small garden, a jar of pickled green beans, and a loaf of bread. The blanket to spread on the grass covered the top to keep the sun off the food.

Emmalee's heart raced when she opened the door herself to the handsome man in a white suit who'd invaded her dreams last night. "Good afternoon." She couldn't control the giant bubble of joy popping through her heart and spreading across her lips.

Richard offered a small posy as a gift. "I smell those delicious cookies all the way outside."

She'd heard of flowers being given by gentlemen, but never received any. "Lettie's bringing a whole 'nother basket full of them." Accepting the posy of wildflowers, she tucked her nose close and inhaled the light fragrance. "Mmm, it smells like the mountians. Thank you."

"I'm glad you like them. How are you?" He asked.

"Well. And you?"

The scents of cinnamon, sugar, and butter grew stronger as Lettie walked in carrying a huge wicker basket. "You two bumpin' noses again? I swear those moo cows have more to say in the fields than comes outta you two on this front porch." Richard's surprise made the older woman snort. "Let me put those in water." She handed off the basket to Richard, switched a checkered tea towel folded across her arm to cover the cookies, and took the sweet little bouquet from Emmalee.

"Joshua," Richard called his driver. "It appears we are feeding an army."

Lettie started issuing packing orders to the men. To his credit, Richard did her bidding with the help of his driver, loading the two baskets, the blanket, an extra blanket "in case", then the box with the teapot and a large jar of water.

"You'd think we were going on a long journey." He joked with the other man on the stoop as he handed off the last of the picnic fixings.

Emmalee grinned. "No, we prepared to potluck. The ladies said we're all sharing each dish. We wouldn't want to run out now, would we?" She slipped the ruffled blue apron off and hung it over a lower hook on the hall hat and coatrack. "I learned from the committee visit how easy it is to underestimate. There wasn't a cookie left in the house the other night."

"I think you have the best housekeeper and cook in the entire city, Emmalee."

Lettie pinked at the compliment.

Smoothing her hair, Emmalee lifted a fashionable white, wide-brimmed hat and pulled the long hatpin out of the crown. She pinned the hat in place through the topknot of her luxurious pompadour and then let the red ribbons race down the back of her white and navy striped garden suit. A red brooch of enameled roses swooped in an arc on her sharp narrow lapel. Choosing this outfit of patriotic colors, made her feel confident she'd fit into the celebration. But seeing how Richard's eyes filled with admiration, those joy bubbles set to popping again tickling in her very core.

"Joshua," Richard called to his driver. "I believe we're ready." The men handed the ladies into the carriage, passed the parasols to each owner, and then Richard joined them.

Joshua tipped his hat and climbed into his seat, gathered the reins, and clucked the carriage horses toward the Broadwater's grassy grounds.

Their picnic spot chosen, and food delivered to the potluck tables, Richard crooked an elbow for Emmalee. "Care for a full tour?"

"I would love it."

Lettie asked, "Would you like me to come with you, Mrs. Warren?"

Emmalee gave a small shake of her head, "I'm sure all will be well in public. Right, Mr. Lewis?"

"I'll take good care of her, Lettie, I promise."

"No shenanigans."

He laughed. "None."

Richard showed Emmalee the bronze fountain of a boy pouring water out of his boot, the massive indoor plunge with its multicolored stain glass windows and forty-foot boulder waterfall, and bought her a peppermint drop at the candy shoppe inside the natatorium.

Children splashed in the shallows, their happy squeals bouncing and echoing around the cavernous building. Water rushing off the three waterfalls, one at the top and two equally spaced lower, added to the volume indoors. A smaller fountain centered in the pool tossed delightful spires into the air entertaining both the children playing around it and observation deck visitors alike. Long rows of polished paneled wooden doors, complete with frosted glass insets ran along the perfectly placed planked deck.

Emmalee grasped the silver metal of the plunge railing taking it all in. "I can't believe how much is here. Lights behind the falls, my goodness." She marveled at the Moroccan architecture. "I'd heard about the resort, but had no inkling all this existed!" The sounds of those in the plunge mixed with the water

"There's so much more." He leaned a hip against the rail. "Come with me to the paddleboats."

"I don't think that's a good idea." She looked at the steamy water of the plunge. "I don't know how to swim."

"You won't need to. I promised Lettie to take good care of you. She's quite the mother hen."

Emmalee lowered her lashes. If only he could understand. "She's protective and fiercely loyal."

"I see that." His lips pursed as he considered. "It's my professional opinion that you have quite a blessing in your housekeeper and chaperone."

Nodding, she added, "I feel the same. We'd only known each other a short time." Emmalee paused. How much could she share without seeming inappropriate?

"How did you meet?" He waited for her response.

As her attorney, he knew so much already. What did it matter if he learned this small bit? She glanced around them and then lowered her voice. No one else needed to hear. "I came from Missoula, a house there owned by Mary Gleim." When he didn't react in disapproval, Emmalee drew in a breath and continued. "The owners, Mary and Chicago Joe, trade girls to keep their, uh, clientele interested and entertained. Lettie had been at a different establishment of Mary's, but she was no longer getting many clients. She sent us both to Helena at the same time, me to continue and Lettie to be the housekeeper."

"That sounds awful."

"It was a wonderful blessing for Lettie. She'd watched a good friend die of morphine overdose."

Emmalee laid a hand on her heart. "Too many girls chose that way out of the trade. For Lettie, she could survive."

A mother and her children tossed a ball in the middle of the pool. One of the children missed the toss. It landed near them with a splash.

Richard took Emmalee's elbow to guide her toward the door and away from accidental eavesdroppers. "You couldn't be a cook or a housekeeper, I take it?"

She walked with him toward the exit, not meeting his eyes. "No. I'm still too young. I'd have been considered a distraction. As an…entertainer we paid rent for our rooms. It didn't really matter what room I was renting, Missoula or Helena, as long as I had a roof over my head and food to eat." She shrugged. "It's not a good life, but I had no other means of survival until Charles paid my rental contract off." She finally looked up. "Charles was good to me. I didn't deserve him."

"Emmalee, I'm very glad he helped you leave that life." He turned in front of her, keeping his eyes on hers. "What you didn't deserve was that hardship. You deserve to be loved, protected, and cared for."

"Thank you." What else could she say after all she'd done? No, she didn't deserve anything but it was nice to hear kind words.

Then Richard pointed to the sign as they strolled by the swimming costume rentals. "Look, you can take lessons."

Emmalee quietly sounded out the words on the sign. "Swim…les-sons-for-all-ages." She checked with Richard. "Is that right? Did I read it right?"

"You did." He gave her a stunning smile. "I hear the women's instructor, Delphina Thomas, is quite good. They've even performed water pageants in the plunge for audiences." He pointed at the rock formation. "She's climbed inside to nearly the top. Then she dives in to the beating drums of the pipe and drum corps."

"Oh my, that would be something to see!"

"Maybe you'll come with me again sometime?"

Emmalee peeked from below her lashes. His earnest request tugged at another joy bubble. "Maybe." Maybe she would be able to come out with him to a water pageant before she left. He hadn't made her feel less respected after learning more of her story. In fact, Richard showed compassion and that caring he'd mentioned.

"I'll watch for the next one. If not that, perhaps you'll join me for a meal in the café. The Sharpe's Orchestra plays each evening this summer." He held the door for Emmalee as they left the building.

She smiled without committing. Two invitations in the space of a few minutes. Would it be right to lead him on? She popped her white lace parasol to shade them in the bright July sunshine.

Another couple ascended the stairs. The woman wore a dove gray walking suit with a small, matching hat perched on her elaborately curled updo. Three long peacock feathers curved from the front, over her head, and off the back.

Meeting on the top step, Richard transferred the door duty to the next gentleman.

"Oh, weren't you with the church welcoming committee the other day?" Emmalee held out a hand. "Zelda, isn't it?"

"Yes. Nice to see you again, I'm sure." Zelda's smile didn't quite seem as friendly. "Afternoon to you, Mr. Lewis." She barely touched fingertips with Emmalee. "I do hope all that drama worked itself out." Tucking her hand into her escort's elbow, Zelda didn't wait for an answer. "Shall we?"

He touched the brim of his hat toward Richard and Emmalee.

Richard frowned at Zelda's back as she crossed the short portico and went inside ahead of her gentleman friend holding the door. He shook his head as he offered an elbow to Emmalee. Taking the first of five stairs down, he said, "I'm sorry. That was on the rude—"

The natatorium's giant door hadn't quite closed behind them, Zelda's voice echoed through the crack. "That's the floozy I told you about."

Emmalee froze, a foot poised to descend, and stared back over her shoulder.

"You know, the one the church is taking on as a charity case. Her lawyer said the poor thing wants to be respectable. She can't even read!"

Missing the stair, Emmalee stumbled and pitched

sideways toward the ground. The white parasol sailed several feet in the air. Her eyes flew open as she realized her mistake.

Richard swooped in front to catch her. "I've got you." His arms closed around her waist, stopping her from missing the fourth stair as well.

Zelda's voice faded off. "One cannot pretend..."

The pounding in her ears drowned out everything around Emmalee. She pushed against his shoulders and righted to stand on her own.

"A poor charity case? Is that what you told those women to get them to my home?" She slid her hand to release his arm, but Richard reacted quickly and wrapped his free hand over Emmalee's fingertips.

He'd locked her hand in place on his bicep. "No, don't listen to nonsense like that."

"But I did hear it." She raised a brow. "It's impossible not to listen when it's already been said. Don't worry, I'll be gone before you know it." She yanked at her hand. "If you'll let me go, please." How could she have let her guard down? One afternoon party didn't mean she had new friends. Foolish. She knew that church couldn't be real. No one could really love and accept unconditionally. But it had seemed like the people were genuine. She'd just been fooled.

"Emmalee, I'm not letting you go like this." He moved in front of her on the last step. With the height difference, now he stood face-to-face with her. "Listen to me."

"Mr. Lewis, I understand. A floozy like me can't expect all you God-fearing people to—"

He leaned forward and kissed her right there where everyone could see. Right in public! The warmth of his lips sent sparks to her toes. In the time she'd plied her trade, kissing wasn't a common experience. Of the few she'd had, none felt as sweet and loving as this!

Richard pulled away. "I hope you'll forgive me. But I needed you to know I don't feel the same way as that unfortunate woman." His hand rose to cup her cheek. "She's an odd duck."

"Uh huh." She stared at him, dazed. Attraction she understood. A few of the men in the past weren't as hard to serve as others. But this—this was something altogether different. Who knew? Should she invite him to spend a private evening with her for the memory? One night with a man she chose versus the years of those she wanted to forget. It might be a memory worth the risk.

Then Zelda's nastiness came back to haunt her. She looked toward the natatorium's elaborate entry, undecided. Another vision of eleven boys filing out behind their mama crossed her mind. Mirielle had been a friend. Calista, too. Were they real or did they consider her a charity case?

"Richard," a deep male voice interrupted. "Mrs. Warren, I hope you're enjoying our country's birthday."

Emmalee startled and whipped around to see who spoke.

Thomas Marlow held up the parasol for Emmalee. "Yours?"

She took it from the gracious man. "Thank you."

He stood to the side of them. "Is it possible we'll celebrate more than a legal win with you two?" He tilted of his head and good humor lifted the edges of his mouth. "Mrs. Warren, what will you do when the case is settled? I imagine a celebration of some sort wouldn't be amiss."

Emmalee ducked her head at the unexpected sense of loss. "I'll be selling my home and moving on." Sharing where would defeat a clean break. Emmalee needed to protect the new persona she'd create.

"Do you mean you'd leave Helena?"

"I can't stay here, Mr. Marlow. I need a fresh start without all the painful," she hesitated and snuck a glance at Richard. "...Um, memories."

"I do understand." His disappointment showed. "That will be a sad day for us, Mrs. Warren. Maybe you'll reconsider." Mr. Marlow's eyes moved from Emmalee to Richard. "He'll be a lucky man if you do, you know." He patted Richard's shoulder. "I'd better check to see how things are going inside. Best to you both."

"He's a kind man." Emmalee said. "Such a difference from some others."

"He is. With his busy schedule running the bank

and the Broadwater since his uncle passed. He's involved in several other businesses also. It amazes me that he takes the time to talk so many personally." Richard held out his arm once more. "Will you walk with me? I think we have more to talk about."

Emmalee took in his serious expression. At the very least, she could listen to the man she wouldn't want to forget. "Yes."

CHAPTER 10

USHERED into the largest living room Emmalee had ever seen, she gaped at the sheer size. Arriving early gave her the chance to get comfortable and be familiar with the presentation. An idea Richard suggested on their walk around the Broadwater's grounds.

"It surprises everyone," Mirielle laughed. "Evan knocked down a wall here in the center. We needed the space with all the boys."

"Now I see why you host the floral club meetings." Emmalee spun in a slow circle taking in the high ceiling, three small table and chair combinations, and three small sofas. The floor covered in strategically placed floral hooked rugs. But it was the art on the walls that drew her delight—watercolors of thirty-two flowers, obviously done by children.

"We haven't been meeting long. But with all the

children in school, except our little miss, there's plenty of room." She pointed out a chair near the hearth. "I'm going to sit there. I'd like you to take the seat next to me on my right."

"Are these the nominated flowers?"

"Yes, the school held a contest. The children chose their favorites to paint from the entries."

"Schools can do that?" Emmalee looked over each picture. "Teach art?" She glimpsed over her shoulder.

Mirielle's compassion soaked her words in loving-kindness. "You can learn art too, Emmalee."

There was so much she wanted the chance to learn. "I always wanted to know how to paint. I've never touched a paintbrush." She crossed the long room to Mirielle. "That's something I'd like to do. Someday."

"Someday happens because you plan for it." She handed a dossier to Emmalee. "Just like you've planned for today."

Opening the official club notebook on the Bitter-root, Emmalee exclaimed, "It's real!" She gently lifted a dried flower. "Even pressed, I can see how lovely it would be."

As Mirielle let in more guests, Emmalee replaced the delicate Bitterroot in between the pages. Then before the ladies claimed the chairs nearby, she quickly slid her dossier under the pile. A small contingent near the door stood chattering as kitchen chairs were brought in by Mirielle's staff to handle the overflow. With two newly formed rows, another eight arrivals found seating.

A few moments later, the room full of club members, Mirielle stood in front of her seat and called the meeting to order. To her right, Emmalee waited to assist as they'd arranged during the picnic.

"Welcome all—and a special welcome to our new members." Mirielle led a round of handclapping for the new members, directing hers toward Emmalee. "It's my pleasure to announce that our founder, Mrs. Mary Long Alderson of Bozeman has set a date for a statewide vote for the Montana Floral Emblem Association. Our special guest has just arrived as Mrs. Alderson's emissary. She's asked for a few minutes to share a note from the association headquarters. Then we'll pass out the nominated floral dossiers to volunteers to share the merits of each flower."

At Mirielle's gesture a young woman, with the same ash brown hair as Emmalee's, stood from the back row and made her way forward. She wore a simple white shirtwaist, no lace or ruffles, and an A-line brown walking skirt. Even her belt spoke of her modest manner. Her only adornment a large crucifix around her neck.

She had a familiar look. But the elegant carriage didn't match the scrappy, disheveled eight-year old Emmalee had left with the nuns in Butte. After ten years, it couldn't be this swan-like creature. The odds that her sister would—no. Wishing for someone didn't make them magically appear any more than wishing away her humiliating past would make it disappear.

"Miss Paulina Graham, you have the floor."

The polite applause didn't drown out the pounding heart in Emmalee's ears. "Paulina?"

Paulina stopped in the middle of the room at the sound of her name. Searching the faces circling the front of the room, her brown eyes connected with Emmalee's and widened. "Emmie?"

Emmalee rose, entranced by the authenticity of her daydream.

The silent surprise around them lasted a mere split-second replaced by the hum of curious whispers.

"Do they know each other?"

"Oh dear." Zelda's voice carried. "Now what kind of scandal will she cause?"

Emmalee jerked as if a slap knocked her backwards. She'd forgotten she had so many witnesses. She blushed and scanned the rows of women. What could she say? Already the social judges began condemning her disruption.

Paulina rushed forward and clasped Emmalee to her. "I found you! I've been praying for so long and my prayers have been answered!"

Though she could see them staring, Emmalee couldn't keep the bottled emotions from breaking. She wrapped Paulina in her arms and wept. "Little Paulina. I've missed you so every day." She lifted her head as tears poured. "You turned out as wonderful as I hoped. I so hoped life would be good to you and Jesse."

"Jesse entered the priesthood a few years ago."

A surge of loving pride rushed to Emmalee's heart. "He always was a good boy. I'm happy for him."

The buzzing grew louder with the inquisitive comments of nearly forty women. "Is that her daughter?"

"No, couldn't be. Look how close in age they are."

"Is it her cousin? Maybe her sister?"

Hands on her sister's shoulders, Paulina held Emmalee away. "You're so beautiful. Just like I remembered."

"I half-hoped you wouldn't remember. But I'm glad you did." She offered a poignant smile. "I only wanted you to be happy, not have sad memories."

Zelda's nosiness broke through their reunion. "What's she mean by that?"

"Shh," another woman hissed. "I'm trying to listen."

Emmalee turned to Mirielle. "I'm sorry to have caused such a commotion." She shook her head in disbelief. She waved a free hand, the other wrapped around her sister's waist. It took a few attempts to get more words past her clogged throat. "This is my little sister. We haven't seen each other in a long time."

Mirielle exchanged glances with Calista, a few chairs away. They both joined the sisters in the center of the room. "It appears we have just witnessed a joyous reunion." Mirielle spread her hands out to include the gathered attendees.

"What a special blessing that all of us could be part of it." Calista added.

Hugging Emmalee, Mirielle whispered in her ear. "My husband was reconciled to his son just two years ago. Such a rarity out here in the west. I'm thrilled for you."

As the crowded room exploded into congratulatory applause, Emmalee said, "Please, Paulina, have your say. All these people came to hear you." She took her seat. Nothing could happen today that would take the joy from this moment.

Everyone settled in again, though a new level of energy enveloped the room.

Paulina looked at her sister, then back at the rest of the audience. "And I thought I brought exciting news from Mrs. Alderson." Light laughter rippled through everyone.

She seemed to collect her thoughts. "I didn't realize a wonderful surprise would be waiting here for me." She placed a hand over her heart. Then she opened a letter, folded in three sections, and read the contents. "Dear constituents," she glanced up for a second. "Since the Montana Floral Emblem Associations inception this past January, so many have diligently worked to bring us to this point. We have finally come to a time of decision. Ladies and gentlemen, the statewide referendum is upon us. All ballots must be returned to the office in Bozeman by the first day of September. It's with deep gratitude that I say thank you for your much needed support. Sincerely, Mrs. Mary Long Alderson."

Cheers rang out as everyone rose for a standing ovation.

Paulina grinned as she announced, "I've brought ballots and membership invitations to encourage civic participation. Our most pressing need is participation in the selection process."

Emmalee found herself caught up in the revelry. The Helena chapter, bursting the wall seams, certainly wouldn't fit in Mirielle Russell's home much longer.

"I'll be staying in Helena this week to help your club expand and register voters. If you haven't registered, or know someone who'd enjoy being a part of such an historic event, I've brought quite a few Montana Floral Emblem Association membership packets as well. And with that, I'll turn the floor back over to Mrs. Russell." With a quick encouraging glance at her sister, Paulina returned to her seat.

"Thank you, Miss Graham. This is such exciting news." She addressed the members, "Now we learn about the contenders for our state flower. As each lady is assigned a flower, she'll be asked to promote it by reading and then discussing the merits with members." Mirielle signaled Emmalee to pass out the dossiers. "We'll give you a few minutes to view your assigned flower."

The busy buzz filled the room again as ladies opened and familiarized themselves with the contents of each flora contender Emmalee passed around.

The volunteer readers agreed to present alphabetically. That put Emmalee among the first to share her presentation. As she walked to the center, Zelda called out, "Do you need a reader, dear?"

Did that woman ever shut up? Emmalee pressed her lips together to avoid spouting back at her least favorite person. Another life she'd learned from coping with rough personalities. Avoid an argument by refusing to engage in one. The last thing she needed in front of her sister would be to humiliate herself by acting like a shrew. "No, thank you."

"She can't read, you know." Zelda informed all those around her, none too discreetly.

Emmalee's hands shook as she opened the dossier. With a deep breath, she read, "The bitterroot is a rose-pink perennial about two inches wide." She took another shallow breath to calm her jittery stomach and chanced a peek at the listening audience. Zelda's astonished face was worth it. Emmalee pushed through her nerves. "It blooms May through June and is found in mountainous terrain of the Rockies. The Natives have peeled and boiled its root for food for many generations. One bag of the bitterroot's ground powder can be traded for a horse because of the nutrient dense value can sustain life in rugged situations. Discovered and catalogued by the Lewis and Clark expedition, this flower carries Meriwether Lewis' name—"

Latin! Don't panic. We practiced the name. But Emmalee couldn't remember it. Sound it out. It starts with the explorer's name. *Lewisia Rediviva.* Starting slowly, she said the part she recognized. "Lew-is..." She remembered! "...i-a Re-di-vi-va." She let out a slow breath and raised her eyes to the crowd. "It means resurrection."

Mirielle asked, "In what you read, Emmalee, why do you think the Bitterroot should or should not be chosen as the state flower?"

"I know all this information is good to know. I even understand why so many other beautiful flowers would represent Montana well." She lifted the pressed bitterroot from the folder. "But the bitterroot is also called the resurrection flower." She turned it in her fingers admiring the dried bloom so carefully preserved as she displayed it for all to see. "I've had a second chance or I wouldn't be here today. That's why this flower has a special place in my heart. But think about Montana. We, as a people, have been denied statehood and yet here we are only a new state younger than most of your children."

Nods and whispers of agreement encouraged Emmalee to finish with passion.

"Here we are living a new life as a state when we'd been denied that for so long. When we were told Montana didn't deserve to be included with the rest of society. She was too rough and not considered respectable." She laid the flower back in the wax paper and closed the dossier. "We have earned the right to be included and deserve the respect due as a state of the union. Second chances seem to be exactly what Montana is about for her people."

Enthusiastic applause rippled around her. One voice cut through the sound. "Was she talking about herself?" Zelda asked.

Richard arrived red-faced and a bit out of breath. "Please forgive the interruption. I need Mrs. Warren to come with me as quickly as possible."

Emmalee threw a distressed look to her sister.

"Go. I'll be here when you get done." Paulina said.

CHAPTER 11

"Steven Brown has been caught forging your mark at the bank." Richard talked as he guided Emmalee out to his carriage.

"He what?"

Mirielle's housekeeper ran after them. "Your parasol, Mrs. Warren."

"Thank you. Oh, I forgot my—"

He captured the parasol and tossed it up onto the black leather seat in one smooth motion. "Would you let Mrs. Russell know I'll be by for anything else Mrs. Warren may have left once we've settled this business?" Richard handed her up the step and bounded up beside Emmalee. Reins flicked, he drove them as quickly as he could from the mansion district, down the sloping road, into town.

"The sheriff wants to see you, the injured party, immediately. Because of the nature of his crime, and being caught in the act, Steven Brown may be going to jail for a long time. The judge has agreed to hear the case if everything is in order before the close of day."

"You told me to delay him as long as possible. I managed to be away from home instead of meeting him the second time." Emmalee's hand held her favorite hat on her head. Long ostrich feathers flapped as if they'd lift off and carry her.

"You made the perfect choice. It forced him to act on his intentions."

"Did they catch him with the mine deeds?"

He slowed the horses enough to turn the corner onto Main.

She slid across the seat and landed hip-to-hip. Righting herself, Emmalee scooted a few inches away and held onto the side of the carriage with one hand while still clamping her hat down in the other.

Richard tossed her a swift answer. "No. The deed to your home signed over to him by forging the capital "E". The county clerk knew to watch for your signature, not a mark."

A few moments later, Richard pulled the horses to a halt. "Frankie, over here." He called to the lanky boy. "Would you please take care of the horses down at the livery and settle up with me in an hour?" He jumped to the ground tossing the reins.

"Sure thing, Mr. Lewis." He caught the reins mid-air and clambered up to drive the rig the few blocks.

Richard checked the clock hands on the courthouse. Still time. He raised his hands and locked onto Emmalee's small waist. No whale bones cinching her mid-section. A woman with a natural hourglass figure not caused by an overly tight corset. He swallowed—hard. "We made it."

"Now that was an exciting ride."

He swung her down.

She didn't stumble. She landed with confidence and grace, holding his shoulders for insurance. Emmalee gave him a look of absolute trust.

For a split second everything in his brain blanked. Lesson eight. To keep his head, he needed to keep his hands off one shapely Emmalee Warren. Until after the court ruled and she wasn't his client any longer.

CHAPTER 12

BRIGHT SUNLIGHT BLAZED as they left the courthouse. The long summer days still tricked his mind. It felt more like two than six in the evening.

"Mrs. Warren, your property is restored. What funds remain in Mr. Brown's account are hereby ordered returned." He couldn't hold back the rush of an out-and-out win. He waited for that special smile. Why was she staring at the sidewalk?

"You're still going, aren't you?"

"You know the answer."

"Why?" Richard took her hands in his. "Don't you realize that no matter where you go, you'll always fear someone finding out the truth?"

"No one will know what I've done in my past."

"You will." He captured Emmalee's hands and cocked his head a notch to catch her gaze. "You will. You can't run from yourself or God. You can't run from your memories, good or bad. Don't you realize that's how God uses us?"

She closed her eyes for a moment. When she opened them, she once again regained control. "I can't stay where it's in other people's memories. I have my sister to think about. Some folks just won't let it go." She squeezed his hands. "You saw that at the picnic and at the Montana Floral Emblem Society today. I'll never be allowed to move on here in Montana, will I? Sell it all for me."

Montana? She'd leave the state? "Please don't go." He had to tell her or he'd never get the chance. "Emmalee, I've fallen in love with you. I don't want to let you go."

Emmalee's face blanched and she stepped backward motioning to the gray granite jail across the street. "You can't love me. It'd be like chaining you up in that stone prison. My reputation would bring you down to my level, not the other way around. Soon you'd feel more like I caused the trouble. Then where would we be?" She shook her head again. "God be with you, Richard. I'll carry you in my heart." She tugged her hand from his and turned away.

"Emmalee!" He didn't try to hide the shredding of his heart. He wanted to grab her and shake sense into her. Instead, he followed a few paces and touched her shoulder.

For a moment, she faltered. Without turning

around, Emmalee gave a small shake of her head.
No. And walked away.

"At least let me drive you." If he could get her in
his carriage, get more time to convince her. He
called. "Emmalee!"

She kept walking, head down, away from him.
Her parasol popped open, blocking out the world.

ONCE SHE TURNED THE CORNER, Emmalee let her feet carry her anywhere they would. The tears trickled, but she swiped them away. Love! Anger roared up inside her chest. In all these years, she'd never needed a man to survive. Men took and took from her. They lied, stole, and cheated. Men were coldhearted poor excuses of— Then a twinge of guilt struck. Charles had been a decent and kind man. So kind he'd paid her debt and married a worthless wanton. He could have set her up as his mistress. But he gave his name and what little respectability he had, but Charles never mentioned love. She couldn't even give him a child to pass on that name to repay his kindness. It wasn't his fault Steven Brown took advantage of her.

And Richard who'd done everything in his power to protect a widowed pariah—tears collected again as her heart squeezed the breath out of her lungs. She grabbed a stair railing, knuckles white, as the spasm wracked her body. Emmalee crossed herself as an apology to the God that might exist for lumping two good men in with all those others she'd known—before. Those who saw her as a product to purchase, use up, and throw away. But love? Maybe that word meant loyalty or caring about family enough to go—

Her hand closed. She held a fist over her heart as she bowed into the pain. She had to leave for everyone's sake. Richard didn't need a tarnished tart ruining his business. Paulina didn't need a reputation because of a soiled sister. She'd probably caused enough damage at the floral meeting. Why had she blurted out their relationship?

"Emmie?"

Why can't people just let me be? If you and I are going to be friends, Lord, then maybe it's time for you to show up and—

"Emmie, it's me, Lily." A hand covered hers on the railing. "Are you all right? Do you need to come in for a rest?" Lily stood one stair up, in front of the side entrance to the grand building. "Oh, you're comin' back. I heard your man passed on."

She'd walked all the way to the Coliseum Theater. A dog returns to his vomit. "No." This pain she deserved for all her bad ways. Not winning back her money, mine, and home. Emmalee Warren definitely didn't deserve to be loved—or to love. But her body was her own now. "I mean, yes, I'm fine." She jerked her hand out from under Lily's and moved out onto the sidewalk. Whether she deserved it or not, the court win meant she had a choice, unlike Lily. Like the bitterroot's resurrection ability, compassion bloomed for women stuck scratching out an existence. "Sorry to trouble you, Lily."

"Hey," she lifted her chin. "The doc checks me monthly. I ain't got all diseased, you know." Lily plopped her hands on the cinched waist of her red satin bustier. Red and black ribbons dangled off the bustier and danced around her black lace skirt in the warm breeze.

"I didn't mean to insult you." Emmalee's raspy throat scratched out. "I'm just…just having a hard day."

"What's so hard for you now?" She narrowed her eyes. "From here it looks like you gots yerself a nice life while I still gots me all this wonder." The sarcasm dripped like a rusty bucket.

"Can I help you?" Emmalee dug in her tan reticule that matched her linen walking suit. She'd chosen the most demure, respectable outfit for court. Anything to pretend to be a decent woman in public. She could at least be a decent person in her own heart. She had enough in her bag so Lily could take a day or two off. "I can give you money you don't have to earn."

"What good would that do me? I ain't got no way to keep earnin' it and I don't take no charity. I pay my taxes." She folded her arms. "I ain't got no schoolin', you know that. That little bit you want to give me ain't gonna git me outta here, now is it?" She lifted her foot to the next stair showing her knees to the world through the widened ruffle slit. "Nice seein' you, anyway, Emmie."

Charles, Mirielle, Calista, and…Richard had helped her. Each one offered from their own experience. She could help Lily. She had the experience of getting free from this life. "Wait!" Emmalee picked up her skirt and caught up to Lily. "Wait, please."

"I gotta go get ready for tonight. You go on now to yer pretty little house in yer pretty clothes. Us workin' girls gotta work."

Taking Lily's hand, Emmalee held her from going through the door. "I really might be able to help, if you want me to."

Lily glanced at the physical contact and twisted her lips to the side as if unsure. "I don't get ya."

"What if I could help you learn to read, and, well…and start over?"

She tipped her head sideways. "Why would you?" Lily pulled her hand away.

"Because I've been where you are—and I know how to get out." She had plenty of money with a producing gold mine. What if she could do that for more women who wanted a better life? "I could help other girls, too."

"You sure you ain't settin' up competition?" She laughed. "Since the silver crash there ain't been enough business around town. Even us fancy ladies—"

"Lily, you know me. We're friends. I'd never do that."

"All right, what's yer high falootin' idea, then?" She challenged Emmalee.

Emmalee nodded, the idea still forming in her head. "Let me buy your rental lease."

"So I owe you then." She shook her head. "I ain't got no way of payin' you back."

"You don't have to." Richard! "I'll have a lawyer draw up a contract that says you're clear and free."

"You'd do that?"

"There's this church," she said. "I met some people there who taught me to read and write. They'll help you, too."

"That's funny." Lily grinned. "We go traipsin' in a church and the place will burst into flames."

Emmalee clapped a hand over her mouth to avoid a snort. Dropping her hand, she said. "That's what I said when Lettie talked me into going."

"Lettie, huh?" A fond expression lit up Lily's face. "I miss that old girl."

"I don't know how to say it the way the preacher did." Her brows drew together. "But bein' religious doesn't matter unless you live like you believe it. He said religion without love is dead."

"Well some of them fuddy-duddies are sure stuffed full of dead religion!"

Emmalee laughed again. "Yes," Zelda's mean spirit came to mind and she sobered. "But maybe those folks are as bad off as we are if they go around knocking other people down all the time. What if God is real? I wouldn't want to be one of those fakes and get called out in front of the Almighty on my last day."

Lily laughed. "Yeah, well I think those folks still have a better chance than one of us." Her eyes narrowed in question. "Why are you bothering to go to a church? There ain't no use for girls like us in a place like that."

Why did she? Emmalee searched her heart. "Some of the people became friends. They didn't ask anything in return. Seems like that kind of faith might be real." She looked up the tall building. Even here, God could see her. "They believe the Lord loves us." Surprised at her own words, Emmalee added, "I want to believe someone loves me. Don't you, Lily?"

"You know how it is. I can't go soft now. It'd destroy me." Then she gave her friend a pitying look. "Oh, poor thing. You went soft, didn't you?"

Happy thoughts welled up in Emmalee at Lily's words. Yes, her heart had softened and let people in. People she cared about more than herself. She smiled at the memories of Mirielle and Calista tutoring and expecting nothing in return, the banker watching out for her accounts, the judge granting justice, Richard asking her to stay—knowing her past and still asking.

A slow dawning rolled through her like a fortress

wall crashing down. God, I think I understand how you loved me through other people. I think I see Lily how you see me—and she's worth saving, isn't she? "I think real religion means God loves us even if we don't deserve it. Then because he does, maybe we show that to other people so they can feel loved, too." She reached out a hand. "Will you let me help you the way my friends helped me?"

Lily searched Emmalee's face. "What if it don't work?"

"Is it working for you now, alone? I kept trying to learn to read and write." Emmalee shrugged. "I failed alone." She refused to back down even if her hand hung in the air for an hour. Face-to-face with what she was, Emmalee finally understood what Richard tried to tell her. True religion wasn't running from the past. True religion is letting God use her broken past to help someone else.

"You can read and write?"

"I can." Come on, Lily. Please. "Do you want to learn?"

Nodding, Lily shook hands with Emmalee. "Yes."

CHAPTER 14

THE CLOCK CHIMED A DIRGE. Richard leaned
into his fist on the desk. Eleven. How could he have
read the situation that badly? The minutes dragged
on for Richard as if pulling the town trollies with a
child's pony instead of electricity. Time slogged since
Emmalee left him at the courthouse. The clouds
blocking sunshine didn't help his mood any. The
farmers would appreciate a late summer rain before
harvest, but Richard's dreary spirit didn't.

A dull shadow moved against the frosted glass of
his office door. A new client might keep his mind
busy at least. He pushed his chair away from his
desk as the first rap rattled the inset window.

"Richard?" Emmalee peeked her head in. "Are you
busy?"

The roar in his blood stung Richard's fingertips.

He could hear his heart gallop against his eardrums. If he wrapped his arms around her, would she run?

She raised her eyebrows. "Are you?"

"Am I what?"

"Busy."

"No, no." He opened the door wide. "Please come in."

She wore the same rose printed ruffled dress when they met. Simple ruffles at her shoulders with pink roses dappling the outfit along her slim figure. When Emmalee dipped her head in response, the wide brim blocked his view. A view Richard very much wanted to study right now as he scrambled to hold the chair for her. He might not get to see her again. Why had she come?

Hooking her white lace parasol on the edge of his desk, Emmalee perched, much like her umbrella, on the chair. She seemed ready for flight.

"I wasn't expecting you." But I'm glad you're here. Richard sat, not taking his eyes off her. He cleared away the piles of paper, shuffled repeatedly the last few days, for the preparation to sell Emmalee's prop- erty. Did she realize he hadn't moved on it? "How can I help you?"

She smiled with an inner beauty, taking his breath as if the wind blew across a candle. The new depth in her eyes drew him in. Emmalee's peaceful, calm spirit mesmerized him. Shedding the worries of her case worked wonders for her.

She cleared her throat. "Richard, I know I said I

was leaving." She folded her hands in her lap, one on top of the other. "But I've had both a change of heart and a change in my legal needs."

Change of heart. What did that mean?

"I ran into, uh, a friend after leaving the courthouse." She swallowed. "I met Lily, one of Chicago Joe's girls I used to, uh, I used to—."

Richard shook off a shiver of relief the friend wasn't another man. Emmalee came to his office, to him. Maybe the other woman had gotten herself into some kind of trouble. "Someone from your past."

"Yes. I tried to give her money, but she wouldn't take it." She glued her eyes on his face. "I want to help her with more than pocket change."

"Go on."

"I know this sounds outlandish, but can you draw up a contract I can use to purchase Lily's room lease?"

"You want to buy her freedom from Chicago Joe?" He had to point out the obvious. "Emmalee, if that's the only profession she knows then this Lily isn't going to have the means to pay you back. You know that, don't you?"

"I don't want to be paid back, Richard." She leaned forward. "I want to give Lily the same opportunity I was given. She wants out. The only way out is a sponsor and an education. I aim to be that sponsor, but Lily won't leave without proof that I'm not going to hold debt over her head."

"Oh." He nodded. "I see." Emmalee's generosity

and desire to help Lily must be her change of heart. She'd never mentioned assisting other women out of that life. The Lord worked wonders bringing amazing accomplishments out of disastrous pasts. If Emmalee could be the bridge for Lily, then he could only imagine what God had planned for these women.

"So you'll help me with that contract?"

"It would be an honor, Emmalee."

She blinked back bright tears. "Thank you. I'll pay whatever you need."

If she was willing to give the funds to free her friend, he could trust and donate his talent. "I don't need money to do this for you and Lily." That still left a question between them. "Will you take her with you then?"

She bit her lip. "I thought a lot about what you said."

"I said a lot of things, Emmalee."

"Yes, well, about not being able to outrun God… or myself. I read Psalm 25." She fiddled with the parasol handle hanging off the desk. "I might be able to do more good here if you haven't begun the sale process." She raised her eyes from the desk and met his. "I'd like to provide a home for women to get an education and start a new life. To release them from distress and shame. To give other women a chance at a life they choose."

"You're staying?" Hope broke through the dark curtains across his heart.

A slow smile spread across Emmalee's lips. "Yes, if you'll help me."

As her words penetrated his skull, Richard stood and walked around his desk. He held out his palm. Emmalee placed her fingers in it and stood with him.

"I will do all within my power to help you create this ministry. But Emmalee, I have a request."

She licked her lips. "Do we need to sign a contract for—"

He drew her hand to his chest and covered it with his own. "Would you consider a more permanent arrangement between us?"

She tipped her head and her brows drew together. Emmalee's gaze fastened on his mouth.

He wanted to kiss her, but held back. "We need a license."

She whispered, "Oh, I didn't realize a home for women—"

"A marriage license."

She stared at Richard. "You want to marry me?"

"Yes." He lowered his head as he gently met her lips.

"My home is going to be full of women with ruined reputations."

"I know."

"People are going to gossip about all of us, about what we've done."

He wrapped his arms around her waist. "No, people are going to say that a very courageous woman is leading other women out of desperation."

"I can't have children." She lowered her lashes. " You should marry a girl who can."

"I think we'll have our hands full enough with the ministry we're starting."

"But—"

"You do remember you're talking to a lawyer trained in rebuttal, don't you?" He put his fingers under her chin and lifted her face. "I do believe God's plans for us will be fulfilling."

"Even if it's helping fallen women and their children?" But she didn't break eye contact with him.

"Women we help that have children who aren't born or raised in a bordello? Emmalee, lives around us matter. Together, we're not only stronger but we can share enough love that the families around us will be stronger, too."

"You want to marry me." Her eyes filled with wonder.

"If you'll have me."

"Yes."

EPILOGUE

S EPTEMBER 1, 1894

M IRIELLE STOOD IN THE CENTER OF HER
great room. "Ladies and gentlemen, the final votes
have been counted. Mrs. Alderson has again sent
Paulina to share official news." She relinquished the
floor.

Paulina untied a ribbon from a decorative scroll
and unfurled it. She peered over the edge with a
teasing grin. "With great pleasure, it's my honor to
reveal," she took a pause building anticipation. "The
bitterroot is the flower you've chosen to take its
rightful place as the state flower of Montana." Oohs
and ahs tittered around the room. "This lovely perennial had a clear win of 3,621 ballots out of 5,857.
The evening primrose and the wild rose were the

closest, both nearly 3,000 votes below the bitterroot."

Richard stood in the back applauding with the rest of the enthusiastic crowd. Beside him, his fiancé clapped with delight—and beside Emmalee, Lily watched the proceedings with awe. "All this pomp for a flower?" she whispered.

"Wait until you read all the newspaper articles and the club dossier on just how special this flower is to the state." Emmalee answered.

"I can't wait to read!"

"On behalf of the people of Montana, Mrs. Alderson has already drafted a letter to the legisla-ture. If all goes as expected, our flower will be official Montana state floral emblem in the very near future. Thank you to all of you."

"Thank you, Paulina." Mirielle returned to lead the club's meeting as Paulina moved through the chairs to stand with her sister. "We have another celebration pending as well. I can't think of a more fitting time to announce it since she championed the bitterroot for us here in Helena." All eyes turned toward Emmalee. "Our very own bitterroot bride, Emmalee Warren, has accepted Mr. Richard Lewis' proposal of matrimony. Let's wish them the very best. Congratulations!"

"Well I'll be—"

"Yes, Zelda?" Emmalee smiled graciously at the flustered woman.

Paulina wrapped an arm around her sister's waist. "I'll be the maid of honor. I'm so excited!"

Richard pressed a kiss to Emmalee's hand. "And I'll be one very happy man to have a wife so deserving of praise. Don't you agree?" He waited ever so patiently, as only a lawyer could, for Zelda's response.

Her eyes darted between the trio. "Yes, yes of course you will. Congratulations."

The crowd closed around them with wishes of joy and good health.

EMMALEE SIGNED HER NAME TO THE marriage license with Paulina and Lily witnessing. The overflowing parlor boasted the Montana Floral Emblem Club as wedding guests, including a few new members—Lily, Rose, and Iris who sat under the mothering eye of Lettie.

"Presenting Mr. and Mrs. Richard Lewis." Jesse, as guest clergy, announced.

"I can't believe we're married." Emmalee smiled into Richard's eyes.

"Now you can practice signing your new name on all the thank you notes." He motioned to the gift table covered in a lovely double damask Irish linen cloth embroidered with little pink and lavender bitterroot blooms around the hem. The tall mound of gifts overflowed onto the ground.

"Emmalee Lewis." She raised up on her tiptoes

and kissed him. "I think it sounds very elegant. Exactly how do you spell that?" She winked.

*O*N *F*EBRUARY *27, 1895* THE *M*ONTANA LEGISLATURE *signed Montana Code, Title 1, Chapter 1, Part 5, Section 1-1-503 into law. The bitterroot symbol popped up on stationery, posters, silverware, and double damask Irish linen. But please remember, bitterroot—not bitter root, or if you prefer, Lewisia Rediviva!*

Bride of
the Rockies
Queen of the Rockies—Book 5
Angela Breidenbach

Bride of the Rockies
Chapter 1

There be three things which are too wonderful for me, yea, four which I know not: The way of an eagle in the air; the way of a serpent upon a rock; the way of a ship in the midst of the sea; and the way of a man with a maid. — Proverbs 30:18-19

MAY 1, 1893

BETTINA GILBERT GAWKED AT THE WHITE City from a bench on the hurricane deck of the steamship as she balanced a sketchbook on one knee, a white lace glove in her lap to avoid graphite smudges. The clouds clearing from their early morning drapery drew away as if a cord were pulled on a stage revealing the glow of bright white classical structures gleaming in the spring sun. Heaven might as well be laid out before her. The Peristyle's forty-eight Roman columns, one for each US state, and its gateway arches spread the massive colonnade across the park's waterway entrance butted by the mammoth casino on one side and the matching music hall on the other. From the distance, the shape made by the harbor buildings seemed more like

Bettina pictured the Lord's giant throne room, regal and triumphant, calling believers into His presence.

Could she capture that sense of incredible royalty in a sketch before the boat docked? The cacophony of the crowd on board rumbled with unencumbered excitement to discover the Columbian Exposition of 1893. The noise of the crowd on the pier walkway rolled across the short distance to collide with the clamor on the boat as if one hand met the other in wild ovation. Did the angelic chorus sound as loud? God must have rather the regular headache. Bettina pressed lace clad fingertips to her temple.

"Beautiful from this vantage." The expressive awe in the man's words tickled her ears, a calm center in the explosion of buzzing energy. His voice soothed her spirit like the sun on her shoulders eased the shivers after the morning's rainy start. "We're blessed with unusual opportunity."

Against the rising roar from inland, where thousands upon thousands listened to President Cleveland's opening address near the Court of Honor's Columbus fountain, and those on the dock scurried to see the great man press the golden key to open the fair, this man's quiet words subdued Bettina's frayed nerves. "Yes, astonishingly so." She slipped the sketch pencil into her hair and turned into the sun, barely escaping its cloudy curtains, to find her fellow passenger.

Lifting her gloved hand to block the glare, Bettina caught a glimpse of a mustache and dark hair under a bowler as she waited out the signal bell clanging orders to the steamship's crew. Then a woman with several well-dressed children, girls in matching gray frocks and boys in matching gray knickers and vests, jostled into an open space hindering a good view of her congenial companion.

He must have given way—as a gentleman should according to her father. Refreshing since manners seemed sorely lacking as more and more travelers bore down on Chicago the last few weeks. Well, it'd been a pleasant interlude amongst the din. She returned to her sketching.

"Antoine, qu'est-ce que je dis? Votre frère... "

French. Bettina tried to ignore the poor mite's scolding for shoving a sibling, but her love of language and sense of unrequited adventure meant a tiny bit of intentional eavesdropping. Poor bored Antoine was picking on his brothers. She knew exactly what that felt like. Her pencil flew. The boy's face, eyes full of longing, took over the upper corner of her page watching the city from afar.

Who were all these people? What were their home countries like? Why were they here, specifically? She loved digging into the details, but on a much more minute level. The magnitude of the crowds everywhere she looked already drained her people patience. She'd much prefer peeping into a microscope or testing soil samples. But then, she still had to find a way to meet the man she hoped would have a place for her to continue her research.

Dr. Kelsey would be here, at the exposition, taking part in the congresses before massive audiences. She couldn't arrive on that day and expect to be prepared. No, coming early to investigate was a wise choice.

She cast a quick, consolation glance at the boy who wanted to be done with the waiting. It had to be harder still to wait when the World's Fair seemed only inches away and as yet so inaccessible. Would anything be as thrilling for him again in his lifetime? Or hers? The boy turned to face away from his family, nose in the air as if watching a seagull, an elbow popped out and jabbed his little brother setting off another squabble. Then he pretended a wide-eyed innocence as his sibling overacted to the injury, sending his mama into another fit of French scolds.

Oh, no. Bettina rolled her lips inward and tightened them to keep from laughing. Anyone could tell what a finger shaking at a nose meant. How many strangers caught her brothers, or her, acting just this way during childhood? She focused on shading dimension into the numerous arches of the Peristyle rather than be an encouraging party to the French lad's mischievous antics. French boys and Irish-American boys. Not so different. Although she seemed to get away with a few pranks as the middle child to keep her four brothers in line, it was survival as far as she was concerned. Adding an eight-year old sister into the family meant jostling for a new pecking order.

Bettina peeked back at the boy. "I see you." She mouthed at him and signaled between their eyes in case he didn't speak English, he'd understand.

He rewarded her with a knowing grin.

She tipped her pencil to her hat—the silent, secret language of mischievous middles.

His grin grew.

She'd take one-on-one communication any day over parties and crowds. Then she caught sight of another gaze. A little breath wedged in her throat at the handsome stranger's nod of detection. He'd noticed the exchange and joined in the humorous moment. Bettina lowered her lashes and turned toward the dock, a warm blush creeping across her cheeks. She whispered to herself, "No distractions." My, but she liked the confident look of him.

Approaching the already teeming dock doubled the volume and drowned out her ability to think. Today national and international experts began to gather and share scientific discoveries and potential medicines derived from the study of plants. The upcoming congresses promised to educate and entertain on every topic imaginable. Though winning a slot to present her own paper on strategic crop planting for maximum harvest both excited and terrified her. Only the possibility of gaining a position close to home at Oberlin College convinced her parents the summer in Chicago would be worth the sacrifice of letting their daughter go for a short time. But would anyone even want to hear an unknown, let alone a woman botanist, speak on farming techniques? Hopefully one Reverend Doctor F. D. Kelsey and his colleagues. She pushed the anxiety away and concentrated on her plan.

Bettina knew where each one of the featured displays would be housed as well as the illustrious names in botanical science she wanted to meet. She'd gleaned several from research papers at college, and thanks to the detailed articles in the Chicago Tribune for the last year or so, she knew which would be speaking or participating with an exhibit. Sharing her work was less about the audience and more about attracting an expert mentor, preferably the good Reverend Doctor Kelsey, to help her navigate her budding botany career.

The daily speakers in the congresses, where the learned of the world convened to educate and enlighten, held both the key to her future and an example of how she should conduct herself when it came her turn to present. While others took in the sights and exotic experiences like camel rides, Egyptian mummies, and Mr. Ferris' wheel on the specially dubbed Street of Cairo, Bettina intended to expand her horizons professionally by studying the scholars she wished to intern under for an advanced degree. She didn't have time for thrill seeking if the few remaining positions that fit her need for a situation near Cleveland, and her parents, were at stake.

The signal bell clanged its arrival announcement. Closing the sketchpad, she eyed the jam of families, including the French lad still pestering his little brother. The mishmash line flowed out from the stairwell and disappeared down two decks toward departure. That could take a while. A few minutes more to remember the awe-struck moment the White City boardwalk spread like a welcome mat to every nation would be worth the delay disembarking after the mass exodus off the steamboat. But then, she'd visit each botanical and agricultural exhibits first. Of all the places, admiring and studying the leading experts' work at the World's Fair had to be the best opportunity to find a master mentor for a degreed botanist.

Bettina's heart drummed in her ears matching the thrum of the antsy throng. Brilliant minds would walk here this summer. She wanted the chance to meet them, discover unknown species, uses for plant materials, and better ways to manage crops to feed the masses—and one day be considered accomplished among those brilliant minds.

She flipped open the page on her sketchbook again, tucking the loose referral letter from her professor safely in the back pages with her carefully planned list of activities, and tugged the pencil from its mooring under the small purple hat. Flaxen strands floated free of her loose chignon and danced in the breeze over her shoulders as she bent to draft a smart line drawing of her first view from Lake Michigan. Bettina studied the entrancing architecture, ducked again to feather in a little shading for the lagoon, and then shifted on the bench for a better angle to finish the brilliant white, elegant casino left of the pier. The beaux-Art domes on many of the structures seemed similar. She started counting, dipping the end of the pencil as she ticked off each one in sight.

"That's an astounding representation." He leaned over her shoulder blocking the morning sun.

Bettina gasped as she dropped her sketchbook. The blotter slid down her navy skirt and lodged near her boot—until she moved to pick it up at the same time as the ship's paddlewheel chugged, jerking as it reversing direction as it moored alongside the dock. Skittering across the planked decking, still wet from the earlier drizzle, the book careened toward the edge. She stood to give chase.

He shot to the rescue, dropping to a knee and snagging the book by the binding corner before it slid under the boat's rail and over the side. As he rose, the pages blew open and fluttered in the breeze loosing one to float free lifted, lolling on a current.

Her reference letter! "Catch that!" she lurched, arm outstretched, and bumped the handsome stranger into the railing as they both reached for the paper. Her pencil sailed from her fingers and plunged into the waves. She scrambled for a handhold and clutched for the page losing her balance. Her gloved hand slid at the same time as her boot pitching her forward, off her feet, in the direction of lapping water against the hull.

He grasped Bettina around the waist a moment before she tumbled into Lake Michigan three decks below.

She squeaked like a strangled seagull as his saving strength cutoff all airflow.

One arm tight around Bettina, he snagged the errant page from the teasing grasp of the breeze as it blew inward and tipped toward the water as if missing its pencil mate. Setting her back on her feet, he let her loose. "Are you all right?"

Dragging in a deep breath, Bettina clasped the white lace at her throat. "Yes. I don't know what would have happened if you hadn't stopped me." She swallowed as she glanced down at the deep, dark water. "Thank you."

"I'm sorry I caused you such distress during a delightfully peaceful moment in all this hullaballoo." He offered her the page. Miss—" He waited.

Goosebumps erupted as he spoke. "Bettina Gilbert." Was there a nip in the wind?

"Miss Gilbert. I feel I owe you some sort of compensation for damaging your art and for the appalling scare."

The way he said her name with that hint of pleasure in his tone sent little tingles down her spine. "No, please, this is the way I take notes." She meant to make quick eye contact, just to be polite, but that one glimpse led to a smile sparkling in his blue eyes. "I—I'm not an artist." She might not have drowned in the lake but his eyes drew her like a bottomless well.

Dark brown, wavy hair refused to maintain the combed back style of the day in the humidity.

"Notes?" Bettina's admirer brought her attention back to the pad as he thumbed to the pencil drawing of the Grecian columns, domes, and spires on the neoclassical architecture. "That's about as creatively detailed a note as I've ever had the pleasure to view. Wait until you see the art on display at the exposition. I've previewed a few in the Manufacturers and Liberal Arts Building. Your notes could rival many of the exhibits."

Coloring, she shook her head. "I appreciate the kind compliment. I've developed the ability to sketch in order to log my studies as a botanist." She shook her head, but a bemused smile touched her lips. "Not an artist." Holding out her hand, Bettina asked, "May I have my sketchpad back, please?"

Rather than returning it, the man had the gall to take a step away from her. "Might I glance through at a few more?"

"I really wish you wouldn't. Some of my notes are," she paused searching for the right word, "personal. I know it looks like random sketches to you, but those pictures are more like a diary of my thoughts."

His smile disappeared. "My apologies. I meant no intrusion." He gave the scuffed up book back. "Luke Edwards, from Montana. Please to make your acquaintance, though under less than favorable circumstances."

"Pleased to meet you, Mr. Edwards." She gave him a polite nod and shook his outstretched hand with her ungloved one. "I'm sure the circumstances were unavoidable." Sparks tingled in her palm at his touch. She glanced up, back at their clasped hands, and up again. Did he feel the energy, too? Retrieving her hand, she blurted out the first thing that popped into her head. "You don't look like a frontier cowboy." Brilliant observation. Could she take that comment back? "What brings you to the fair?"

"Not everyone in Montana is a cowboy, Miss Gilbert." He pointed to the bench offering to sit with her. "Perhaps you'd let me—" The wind curled its fingers and snatched through his dark hair triumphing in glee as the gust grabbed the bowler off his head and tossed it a goodly distance into ship center. He pivoted to see where it'd blown off to and then back to Bettina, "Pardon me a moment." For a man in a formal suit and starched collar, he dodged nimbly through the shuffling travelers as the boat anchored.

Bettina tried to hold back a grin. But watching the good-looking Montanan dive and resurface amongst the throng reminded her of duck bobbing for fish, albeit unsuccessfully. She shouldn't laugh at his misfortune. But there he was again, bopping up with a hand signal for one more moment. She couldn't help herself. She giggled and pressed her fingers against her mouth. Their eyes connected. For a brief moment, she saw into his heart. Bettina knew something shifted in hers. She lowered her hand to wrap her waist, where he'd held her from disaster and realized she'd lost a glove. Peering around and under the bench, Bettina couldn't find it. She stood to search for her hero. Possibly he'd found it along with his hat? But Mr. Edwards had disappeared in the press of oncoming fair-goers as she was pushed along the ship's railing toward the gangway by the last rush of passengers.

I hope you enjoyed *Flower of the Rockies*, book 4 in the Queen of the Rockies series. I loved sharing a little true Montana history about how our state flower, the bitterroot, came to be through Emmalee and Richard's love story. The early years of Montana's state history could easily be compared to the legend of Camelot. "*For happily ever aftering is here in Camelot…*" Yes, the mists have swallowed up some of our most incredible history, but we won't let it be forgotten.

I wrote six stories that tell some of the special events and what happens as Montana becomes a state in the Queen of the Rockies Series. The next books in the series, *Bride of the Rockies* and *Flame of the Rockies* will complete the set. All six are available in e-book, paperback, and large print editions.

As an author, I love feedback. Candidly, you're the

reason I continue to explore the history of Montana. So tell me what you liked or loved, what questions or thoughts this book brought to mind, or what made you laugh and cry. You can write to me on the contact page of my website. I do answer emails personally. Visit me on the web at: http://Angela-Breidenbach.com or tune into one of my podcasts also easily found on my site. I hope you'll enjoy reading the stories I write and listening to my show.

Finally, I need to ask a favor. Reviews help books sell. Would you kindly leave a review on your favorite site such as Bookbub, Goodreads, Amazon, or any other review site? Your feedback is important to me! Reviews can be hard to come by these days. You, the reader, have the power now to make or break a book.

Thank you so much for reading *Flower of the Rockies*, spending time with the people of Helena, and I hope you'll also enjoy the sample chapter of *Bride of the Rockies*, the fifth in this series at the end of this story. But most of all, thank you for spending time with me. I'll see you in the pages of the next book.

If you'd like to receive new release information, genealogy tips, or keep up with me through my newsletter please consider signing up when you visit my website or you can join at this link:

https://landing.mailerlite.com/webforms/ landing/n0s2t2

Appreciatively,

Angela Breidenbach

P.S. Here's a little about the other books in the first few years of Montana's statehood:

Did you miss the beginning of Frankie and Joey's story in Queen of the Rockies?

What if you were caught doing something good, but the man you loved didn't see it that way? Meet Calista Blythe and Albert Shanahan in 1889…

Queen of the Rockies, Book 1 and kick off title of the series by Angela Breidenbach ~ 1889 (Helena, MT): Calista Blythe enters the first Miss Snowflake Pageant celebrating Montana statehood to expose the plight of street urchins. But hiding an indentured orphan could unravel Calista's reputation, and her budding romance with pageant organizer, Albert Shanahan, if her secret is revealed. Will love or law prevail?

Song of the Rockies. 1890 Montana historical.

What would you do if you were given eleven rowdy street newsies and told either you turn them into model citizens or they get sold into indenture or sent to the military? *Song of the Rockies* is the story of a sweet music teacher, Mirielle Sheehan, and eleven boys given one chance or else! Evan Russell lost everything—his ranch, his wife, and now after trusting relatives with his young son, even the little boy is missing. How can a beautiful symphony of the heart come from such chaos? *Reminiscent of Little Men.*

Heart of the Rockies. 1892 Montana historical.
Could she believe in herself when no one else did?

A progressive thinker in 1892 Montana, Delphina O'Connor believed in God-given dreams for women didn't stop at marriage and children. Hers might not include a husband or family at all. So when Hugh Thomas rescues the new swimming instructor at the elegant Broadwater Natatorium from near drowning in the plunge, how can anyone believe the freedom to enjoy swimming, competition, and a healthy body is an appropriate activity for a proper lady? Hugh is about to find out status quo is the starting line for a courageous woman with a dream!

Heart of the Rockies explores the real-world question: What do you do when you think differently than the world around you?

Would you like to know one surprising thing about Montana that catches most tourists unaware? The amount of art and culture spread across our state is astonishing! Montanans are known for our independent streak. Living in vast areas with some pretty extreme weather can do that to you. But we locals flock to art and cultural experiences en masse.

In honor of our heroine, Emmalee, as she tries to understand society and the "cultured" ladies, let me share a few of my favorite cultural spots with you so they end up on your "not to miss" list when you visit. If you visited Montana and didn't see all the culture, then you didn't really visit Montana. You'll have to come back!

**Top Cultural Experiences
(according to Angie):**
1. **Summer Theatre:** No matter which theatre

you plan to visit, be sure you book well in advance. Seats are notoriously sold out early! Some of my best memories are because of the multitude of cultural experiences.

a. **Big Fork Summer Playhouse** is a delightful extravaganza with a rotation of Broadway musicals, plays, and variety stage shows. Actors come from all over the place. My son, Forrest, worked at this theatre for a couple of summers. We took every family member we could and ran into friends each time. This playhouse is in Bigfork, MT. You'll want to stroll the quaint village shops and play in Flathead Lake to make your weekend complete. Lots of bed and breakfast options, campgrounds, and motels. But like the playhouse, you must book well ahead. For a tiny town, it's incredibly popular for those who are in the know.

b. **Virginia City Players** are another excellent summer theatre specializing in plays and Vaudeville. My son also worked in Virginia City entertaining visitors. This playhouse is quite small, but authentic to the late 1800s. Be sure to book way ahead if you want to stay locally at a bed and breakfast, the authentic hotel, or one mile over you can stay inside the Nevada City living museum after it closes. My dad and I did that while Forrest was an actor with the Virginia City Players. We had a wonderful time wandering the preserved Old West town on our own. Don't miss riding the train between the two towns, taking a ride with the stage coach, and window shopping along the boardwalk where businesses are still exactly as they were abandoned nearly 100 years ago. Catch the reenactments at Nevada City while you're in the area.

c. Lest you think there are only two summer theatre companies… nope! There are quite a few. I'm providing you a link to find so many more. Our state is huge and you may not be able to see it all. But at least you'll be prepared to choose the best summer theatre options.

http://montanalinks.com/arts/theatre/

2. Year-round culture

a. Montana Children's Theater — Disclaimer: If I remember correctly, most of my family (including me) have been in at least one of the MCT shows. The MCT travels around the world introducing school children to plays. But they also present Broadway shows with local talent. I was in Brigadoon (my favorite musical) while the list of shows my kids have performed in is way too long to mention here. Suffice it to say that though the company is world-renowned, we locals consider it our own special secret. Beautiful, modern theater and stage with an amazing costume department.

b. Montana Reparatory Theatre travels widely and performs at the University of Montana in Missoula. Many friends have been in these shows that include Shakespeare. Our U of M Drama School has some quite well known actors that call it their alma mater.

c. Concerts by internationally famous musicians, orchestras, comedy acts, ballet, and special Christmas events are regular happenings. A lot of musicians started here!

d. First Fridays, specialty markets, and craft fairs include artists and art galleries, written and spoken word performances, busking musicians, and local Montana Made crafters. Then, weekly we have the Farmers Market every Saturday in the warm months and certain evenings indoors during the cold months. Our Christmas craft fairs are elbow room only in most venues. Creativity abounds!

3. Food! Most visitors are shocked to find out many famous restaurants started locally in Montana. Have you eaten at HuHot, MacKenzie River Pizza, Jakers, 4Bs (just love the tomato soup!) Yes, there are more but those are off the top of my head. I've been surprised at how many local restaurants have branched out across the country. Though we're all still waiting on the elusive Red Lobster to one day open. That rumor, along with Olive Garden rumors, has been hotly anticipated for at least 25 years. Yet those two restaurants never seem to materialize. Guess our local eateries just have them too intimidated.

We have a joke that we export restaurants to the rest of the country. Except it's really true. Food in Montana is excellent. Each town has its own specialty restaurants, fusions, and down home eateries. We love a good steak, bison burger, and huckleberry shake. But we also love great chocolate. The best is at the Sweet Palace in Philipsburg.

Oh hey, if you read book 3, Heart of the Rockies, then you already know about Fairmont Hot Springs. It's a short drive away from the Sweet Palace in Philipsburg! No one in our family would dare drive anywhere close to the Sweet Palace and not stop. That would be, gasp, an unforgivable lapse in judgement.

Be sure you plan for the fairs August through September as well. Our fair food is, well, you'll hear everyone in town talking about what night of the fair they're going for vikings, tater pigs, and lemondairies.

a. Viking: a deep fried sausage that's been dipped in batter and… the recipe is a secret. But no one would miss a viking at the Western Montana Fair! The line is always curled around corners and down the lane.

b. Tater pigs and tails: baked potato with a breakfast sausage drilled into the middle served with butter, sour cream, and cheese. The tails are the drilled out potato center deep fried to a crisp golden —okay, just a fancy French fry. But I'm sure you'll agree it's perfect dipped in the tater pig toppings.

c. Lemondairy: frozen lemonade with vanilla soft serve. But the best ones are topped with huckleberries! *I've heard of other toppings, gasp, but that's sacrilege!*

Now you're armed with all your activities and local food favorites. Come visit Montana!

If you'd like to have me visit your book club via Zoom, Facebook Live, or another option please let me know. I really enjoy connecting with reader groups. I'm happy to answer questions or give a talk, whatever your group would enjoy. Send me a note via the contact page on my website or email me at:
angela@angelabreidenbach.com

Conversation starter ideas for book clubs:

- What do you wish you learned earlier in your life?
- When did you feel uncomfortable or unwelcome joining a group of people you didn't know?
- Did you feel somehow unworthy?

- Did anyone help you get comfortable in an unfamiliar situation?
- If so, what did they do to help you feel comfortable? How can we use that to help others?
- Is your church welcoming to people who don't know how to dress for or behave in church?
- If someone wants to change, how can we help them in their journey?
- If true love is laying down one's life for another, does it always mean literal death? What else could it mean?
- Who is your favorite character in *Flower of the Rockies*? Why?
- A few of the characters from the other books cross over now and then. Do you have a favorite character from the Queen of the Rockies Series? Who, and how do you relate to that character?
- Books 4, Flower of the Rockies, and 5, Bride of the Rockies, have a timeline that crosses a bit because of simultaneous history. If you've already enjoyed Bride of the Rockies, does reading either one in a different order give you a different perspective of the other one?
- What new historical fact did you learn?
- Did you find an ancestor in the pages of this book? *(If so, please let Angie know so she*

can share any research she's learned about your ancestor.)

- What surprised you about the education levels of the Montana women of the 1890s?
- What do you know about your own state flower or how it was chosen?
- Would you try eating bitterroot if it was offered to you? Why or why not?
- Where would you like to visit in Montana?
- What would you like to do?
- Are you excited for the next book yet?

I hope you find joy in the journey, too!
Angela Breidenbach

ABOUT THE AUTHOR

Angela Breidenbach is a professional genealogist, bestselling author, and a media personality. Angela volunteers as the Christian Author Network's president. As a Montana author, it's one of her favorite places to write about whether historical or contemporary settings. She lives in Missoula with her hubby, two miniature horses, and a fe-lion personal assistant named Muse. Muse can high-five, shake hands, roll over, and jump through a hoop. Surprisingly, Angie can also! You'll likely find both of them on social media creating hijinks.

Connect online:
http://www.AngelaBreidenbach.com
Bookbub/Facebook/Instagram/Twitter/Pinterest: @AngBreidenbach

facebook.com/AngBreidenbach

twitter.com/angbreidenbach

bookbub.com/profile/angela-breidenbach

pinterest.com/AngBreidenbach